A TERRIBLE DEATH

Fargo stared at the old man's body. His clothes were torn and his legs had been shredded to the bone.

But it was the man's eyes that held him. Even in death they still stared out with a terror beyond imagining.

"Something put the fear of God into him," the Trailsman said.

"But what was it?" David Corry asked, looking away from the rotting corpse.

"I don't know," Fargo replied. "But whatever it is it's still somewhere in this forest. And you can bet that it knows we're here, and that it's waiting for us."

⌀ SIGNET WESTERN (0451)

THE TRAILSMAN RIDES ON

- [ ] **THE TRAILSMAN #79: SMOKY HELL TRAIL by Jon Sharpe.** Through a blizzard of bullets and a cloud of gunsmoke ... with a kid he aimed to turn into a man ... with a lady he aimed to turn into a woman ... and wave after wave of killers he had to aim fast to turn into corpses ... Skye Fargo rides the desolate stretch of savage wilderness they call the Smoky Hell Trail. (154045—$2.75)

- [ ] **THE TRAILSMAN #82: MESCALERO MASK by Jon Sharpe.** On a special investigative mission, Skye has to blaze through a tangle of rampaging redskin terror and two-faced, kill-crazy bluecoats to keep the U.S. flag from being soaked in blood and wrapped around his bullet-ridden corpse ... (156110—$2.95)

- [ ] **THE TRAILSMAN #83: DEAD MAN'S FOREST by Jon Sharpe.** When a lady friend is taken hostage, Skye Fargo sets out to hunt down a killer and gets caught in a tangle of sex, salvation and slaying. He soon finds out too much of a good thing can kill a man.... (156765—$2.95)

- [ ] **THE TRAILSMAN #84: UTAH SLAUGHTER by Jon Sharpe.** Skye Fargo rides a road to hell paved with rampaging renegades and lusting ladies. This was Utah, where a man could have as many women as he could satisfy and as much trouble as he could handle ... and the Trailsman was setting records for both.... (157192—$2.95)

- [ ] **THE TRAILSMAN #85: CALL OF THE WHITE WOLF by Jon Sharpe.** When Skye Fargo led the wagon train organized by beautiful Annabel Dorrance into the mountains of Montana, he figured there'd be redskins, outcast bands ready to rape and pillage, and the occasional tussle with Annabel's trigger-happy boyfriend—but he never thought he'd meet a fearsome tooth-and-nail killer! (157613—$2.95)

Buy them at your local bookstore or use this convenient coupon for ordering.

NEW AMERICAN LIBRARY
P.O. Box 999, Bergenfield, New Jersey 07621

Please send me the books I have checked above. I am enclosing $_____
(please add $1.00 to this order to cover postage and handling). Send check or money order—no cash or C.O.D.'s. Prices and numbers are subject to change without notice.

Name_____

Address_____

City _____ State _____ Zip Code _____

Allow 4-6 weeks for delivery.
This offer, prices and numbers are subject to change without notice.

CALL OF THE WHITE WOLF

by

Jon Sharpe

PUBLISHER'S NOTE

This book is a work of fiction. Names, characters, places and incidents either are the product of the author's imagination or are used fictitiously, and any resemblance to actual persons, living or dead, events, or locales is entirely coincidental.

NAL BOOKS ARE AVAILABLE AT QUANTITY DISCOUNTS WHEN USED TO PROMOTE PRODUCTS OR SERVICES. FOR INFORMATION PLEASE WRITE TO PREMIUM MARKETING DIVISION, NEW AMERICAN LIBRARY, 1633 BROADWAY, NEW YORK, NEW YORK 10019.

Copyright © 1988 by Jon Sharpe

All rights reserved

The first chapter of this book previously appeared in *Utah Slaughter,* the eighty-fourth book in this series.

SIGNET TRADEMARK REG. U.S. PAT OFF. AND FOREIGN COUNTRIES
REGISTERED TRADEMARK—MARCA REGISTRADA
HECHO EN CHICAGO, U.S.A.

SIGNET, SIGNET CLASSIC, MENTOR, ONYX, PLUME, MERIDIAN and NAL BOOKS are published by NAL PENGUIN INC., 1633 Broadway, New York, New York 10019

First Printing, January, 1989

1 2 3 4 5 6 7 8 9

PRINTED IN THE UNITED STATES OF AMERICA

The Trailsman

Beginnings . . . they bend the tree and they mark the man. Skye Fargo was born when he was eighteen. Terror was his midwife, vengeance his first cry. Killing spawned Skye Fargo, ruthless, cold-blooded murder. Out of the acrid smoke of gunpowder still hanging in the air, he rose, cried out a promise never forgotten.

The Trailsman, they began to call him, all across the West: searcher, scout, hunter, the man who could see where others only looked, his skills for hire but not his soul, the man who lived each day to the fullest, yet trailed each tomorrow. Skye Fargo, the Trailsman, the seeker who could take the wildness of a land and the wanting of a woman and make them his own.

*1861, the fierce, wild land
in the heart of the Cabinet Mountains
in the northwest corner of
the Montana Territory . . .*

1

The big man with the lake-blue eyes rode slowly, a frown digging into his forehead as he scanned the wild and mountainous terrain, heavy with black oak, mountain ash, and box elder. With his eyes, his ears, and his nose, with the inner senses as well as the outer, he read the land as other men read a book.

On this late-autumn day it was his nose that had alerted him first and sent wariness crawling through his body. Through the sunlit breeze he had caught the odor that did what it always did: make his heart sink with depairing bitterness. He reined the magnificent Ovaro he rode to a halt, and slid to the ground to stand beside the pure white midsection and the jet-black fore and hindquarters. He drew in another deep breath and let his nostrils flare. He began to move forward on foot, the odor growing stronger, a sour, sickeningly cloying scent, and his lips pulled back in a grimace. Parting the leaves on the low branches, he pushed forward carefully and saw the wagon first, a Studebaker farm wagon, highsided and outfitted with tall, thin poles on which to rig a canvas top. It lay half on its side where it had smashed into a tree.

The big man stepped forward more quickly, his eyes sweeping the ground near the wagon. He spotted the woman, or rather what was left of her. Then he found the other bodies lying on the ground, three men and another woman. All were torn apart, each body bearing deep gouges, some half-eaten away, each ravaged, and the ground still stained dark red. His eyes returned to the wagon and he saw that a team of horses had pulled the big rig. One had broken away and dragged part of the shaft with it. The other horse lay on its side, a good part of it torn to pieces. The big man felt the frown dig deeper into his brow as he stared at the grisly remains. Something different, he muttered to himself. Not just more sickening, not just more savage. Different, he repeated, and tried to give words to the thoughts that stabbed at him. He was still pondering when the sound broke into his musings; he spun, the big Colt in his hand, and peered at a thicket of dense, high brush. The sound came again, something between a moan and a breathy gasp.

He moved forward, pushed the tangle of brush aside with his hands, and was halfway through it when he spotted the form lying deep in the thicket. He plunged forward to drop to one knee and heard the muttered oath from his lips as he stared at a child, a little girl hardly more than five or six years old, he guessed. She lay on her back, her wide-open eyes staring upward.

He reached down and carefully drew her up to a sitting position. He saw no marks on her, no bloodstained places on her dark-blue cotton dress. But she was cold, clammy to the touch, as he lifted her.

"It's going to be all right," he said, but she only stared at him with eyes that seemed to see nothing. He took her up in his arms and started to back out through the brush when he caught the sound of horses moving nearby. He dropped down and put the little girl back into the brush. "Just stay there, honey," he said, but saw that she neither moved nor acknowledged him in any way. She was definitely alive but she seemed in some sort of trance.

He turned from the child, flattened himself beside her, and peered out through the brush to see the three horsemen appear. Wearing only breechclouts, sitting astride short-legged ponies, they moved toward the wagon, halted, and dropped to the ground. Skye Fargo's eyes grew narrow and cold.

Not Shoshoni, Fargo murmured to himself. Not Nez Percé, either. He knew both tribes well. Probably Bannock or Flathead, he decided as he watched the Indians begin to crawl over the wagon and pull things from it. One brave with a thick nose had just begun to sort through a jewelry box he overturned when the child emitted another of the half-moan, half-whimpered sounds.

Shit, Fargo swore silently as he saw the three men freeze, then turn toward the brush in unison.

The one with the thick nose hopped from the wagon with catlike grace, landing silently on both feet. Fargo saw him draw the tomahawk from his belt. He moved toward the thick brush, the other two following, flanking him on both sides. Fargo's finger pulled back from the trigger of the big Colt in his hand. There could be others nearby. Shots would certainly bring them. He'd use the Colt only as a last resort. He began to slide back through the brush. He left the child for them to find. It would hold their attention for a moment, and moments were suddenly precious.

He saw the Indians move into the heavy brush, the thick-nosed one with the tomahawk upraised. Fargo, almost prone on the ground, reached his hand down to the calf holster strapped around his leg. He drew out the thin, razor-sharp double-edged throwing knife, brought his arm back to his side, and waited, his eyes on the men. He was ready when they halted in surprise as they came onto the child. They exchanged short, grunted comments in what sounded like a variation of Shoshonean. While their attention was riveted on the child, Fargo whipped his arm up and sent the thin blade whistling through the air. It struck the thick-nosed one at the base of his neck, slamming in to the hilt.

Fargo saw the Indian half-turn, his eyes grow wide, and his mouth fall open. He did a strange one-legged dance as he groped to pull at the handle of the knife and he fell sideways, breath wheezing through his open mouth with a whistling sound.

The other two still stared at him in surprise, that precious moment that could spell the difference between life and death, Fargo knew. He sprang, charged forward through the brush, the Colt held in his one hand. He was onto the two Indians as they spun. He smashed the nearest one across the forehead with the Colt. The man went down as though poleaxed.

Fargo dropped almost to his knees, and the third brave, charging, couldn't pull back. He hurtled over Fargo's head in an out-of-control somersault, landed on his back, rolled, and sprang to his feet. Fargo saw the bone hunting knife in his hand.

The Trailsman backed and the attacker came at him, a short figure holding the knife in front of him. Fargo backed again, cleared the brush, and holstered his Colt. As he did so, with a hissing grin, the Indian charged. He swept the knife forward and Fargo ducked left, avoiding the blow. He almost failed to get away from the sweeping thrust that followed. The Indian was quick, he saw, and he darted to his left to avoid another strike.

The Indian had realized by now that Fargo did not want to use the Colt and he pressed forward with abandon. The Trailsman circled, found himself near the front of the wagon, and bent down to scoop up a broken length of the shaft. The piece of wood, jagged at one end, measured almost four feet in length. Holding it in both hands, clublike, Fargo swung at his foe. The man easily avoided him. Fargo tried another swing, then another, purposefully making it awkward. He watched the Indian easily pull away from both. He swung again and this time he saw the man's eyes watching him carefully, measuring distances, an eager confidence in his tight mouth.

Fargo attempted another clumsy swing and let the brave duck under it easily. Then, with a curse, he let go a roundhouse swing of the club. He saw the Indian wait, time his move, and duck under the blow to charge in with his knife aimed straight forward. He expected Fargo to be off balance, but the Trailsman's leg muscles were tight, his body poised on the balls of his feet. He half-spun and brought the length of shaft up as though he might throw an uppercut. The long piece of wood caught the Indian under the point of the jaw as he came in. Fargo heard the man's choking gasp as he staggered back and came to a shuddering halt. A stream of blood poured down from the wound.

Fargo whirled the length of wood and, wielding it with both hands, slammed it down across the man's skull with all his strength. His opponent toppled backward, and like an eggshell cracking open, a jagged crack of red split his head. He twitched for a brief moment and was still.

Fargo dropped the piece of harness shaft, strode into the thick brush, and pulled the other two Indians out. He retrieved his throwing knife, wiped it clean on the grass, and strode into the brush again where he'd left the little girl. She hadn't moved and her eyes stared without seeing as he picked her up and carried her to the Ovaro.

"Can you hear me, honey?" he asked her. He received no response of any kind. Her staring eyes didn't even blink. He placed her gently against his chest, climbed onto the pinto with her, and turned the horse away from the grisly scene. He rode holding her against him and felt the rhythm of her breathing. Except for that, he'd have thought her lifeless.

Fargo turned the horse down the hill, riding north by east. The town was in that direction and he had been on his way there, anyway. But he had to find it first. He scanned the land below, spotted a deer trail that led downward, and swung onto it. He reached the bottom of the hill, swung north, and held the child tight against him with one hand as he grasped the reins with the other. He had gone perhaps a hundred yards when he saw the three riders moving toward him; he reined to a halt as they approached.

The young woman, gold-brown hair and hazel eyes set in an apple-cheeked, pretty face, frowned at the child he held against him. "You know the fastest way to Mountainville?" he asked, and she nodded. "There a doctor there?" Fargo questioned.

One of the men answered. "Yep, Doc Kerr. Is she hurt?" he asked and gestured to the child.

"More inside then outside, I'm thinking. She's in shock, real deep shock," Fargo said. "I just found her."

"Where?" the young woman asked.

"Up the hills a way. She must've been with the wagon," Fargo said.

"Wagon?" the young woman echoed, her pretty face growing tight.

"We can talk after I get her to a doc," Fargo answered.

The girl wheeled her horse in a circle. "Let's go," she said, and set off at a fast canter.

Fargo held the child tightly to him as he followed, and the two men swung in behind him. The young woman led the way down a steep incline and swerved right when it ended, taking a trail between two long hills thick with mountain ash. At the end of the corridor of hills he saw the town appear and, rising up just behind it, a tall mountain. The town was well-named, he saw, stretching along the very base of the mountain in a long, thin line. The girl led the way to a small frame house at the forward edge of the narrow line of buildings, swung from her horse with easy grace, and reached out to take the child from his arms as he pulled to a halt.

He passed the little girl to her just as the thin-framed man with half-spectacles hurried from the house, gray eyes already taking in the child. "What happened to her?" the doctor asked as he took the child and began to carry her toward the house.

"I'd say she witnessed something pretty terrible. She's the only survivor of a wagon," Fargo said.

"Come see me later," the doctor said.

A woman in a white apron opened the door for him and he went into the house carrying the little girl. She still stared with blank, haunted, unblinking eyes.

Fargo nodded, stepped back, and found the young woman waiting, her hazel eyes serious. He took a proper look at her for the first time and saw full red lips as well as apple cheeks, gold-brown hair hanging softly almost to her shoulders, a combination of strength and sweetness in her pretty face. A darkgreen blouse thrust forward over deep, full breasts, he noted, and she had a narrow waist and rounded hips.

"Take me back to that wagon," she said.

"I don't think you want to go back there, honey," Fargo said.

"I have to go back," she said. "And I'm quite able to face unpleasant things. I've seen the results of an Indian attack."

"This is different," Fargo said.

"Will you take me or must I go searching for myself?" she asked with a touch of asperity.

He shrugged. "If you insist, honey," he said. He watched her swing onto her horse. A nicely turned ankle and calf showed as she mounted, and Fargo saw the two men swing in beside her. One of the men had a long, thin face and graying hair, an expression more usually found on a schoolteacher than a cowhand. The man wore no gun, Fargo noted. The other man was more typical, with a windbeaten face and a single-action Colt belt pistol on his hip.

"I'm Annabel," the young woman said. She gestured to the other men. "David Corry and Hal."

"Fargo," the big man said, and saw the tiny furrow come to her brow at once.

"Fargo?" she repeated.

"Skye Fargo." He saw the quick glance she flung at David, the older man. She returned her eyes to the big man and he saw her carefully compose her face.

"How did you come onto this wagon?" she asked.

"By accident. I was working my way down, looking for Mountainville," Fargo said.

She took in the reply and said nothing more until

they were nearly atop the hill where he'd found the wagon.

"We were out looking for a wagon that was expected a week ago," Annabel said. "We allowed for their being delayed, but when they didn't arrive yesterday, we went looking. We didn't find anything."

Fargo made no reply as he led the way through the trees on the high land, turned, and came onto the place where the wagon lay smashed against the tree. His eyes were on the girl as she stared at the wagon, then at the bodies on the ground, and he watched her face grow chalk-white. "It's the Frawley wagon," she murmured. "Oh, my God, yes. Green Studebaker farm wagon." Her eyes went to the mutilated forms on the ground. "Three men, two women, one child. Oh, God."

Annabel turned her face away and Fargo saw her fight down being sick. "Good God, I've never seen anything like this," she murmured.

"How many have you seen?" Fargo asked.

"Only one," she admitted. "But it wasn't like this." Her eyes went to the three Indians nearby. "At least they got some of them," she muttered.

"I got those three," Fargo said, and her eyes widened at him. "They came along just as I found the child. They were going to scavenge the wagon."

"But they must've been part of those who attacked the wagon," the girl said.

"No," Fargo answered, and she frowned back. "They'd have done their scavenging then. These just happened along, as I did."

"This attack was at least two, maybe three days ago," the man named Hal said.

Fargo nodded and watched Annabel force herself to look at the torn and mutilated bodies, the eaten-away remains of the horse and her apple-cheeked face mirrored horror.

"They were killed by Indians. Animals did the rest," she said.

"Coyotes, maybe wolves," Hal added. "Maybe cougar, bear, raccoon, wolverine—damn near anything that walks these mountains."

Fargo's lake-blue eyes were narrowed as he scanned the grisly scene again. "You see anything different here? Anything strange?" he asked.

Hal shrugged. "Never seen animals do such a scavenging job," he said. "Guess the smell of blood kept bringing on more and more."

"Maybe," Fargo said.

"Maybe?" Annabel frowned at him. "Of course it was animals. What else would've torn them apart this way?"

"Animals did that, all right," Fargo agreed. "But there's something else." He glanced at the others and saw them waiting. "There's not an arrow in any of these poor people," Fargo said, and watched the others slowly turn their eyes to the grisly scene again. He waited as they stared and frowned and finally looked at him again. "Not an arrow in the wagon, either, or on the ground," he commented.

David Corry pursed his lips in thought as he spoke. "Maybe the animals tore away the parts where the arrows were," he offered.

"Every part they tore off held an arrow?" Fargo returned.

"Sort of stretches coincidence, doesn't it?" David admitted.

"Maybe they didn't use arrows in the attack," Annabel said.

"Maybe they came on the wagon by dark and used knives and tomahawks and lances."

Fargo's half-smile was grim. "That's just possible," he said, "but it'd be a damn unusual attack on a single wagon." His eyes grew narrow again. "There's one thing more: I don't see one pony print here except for those three varmints I killed."

"If it was a knife attack, they'd have been on foot," the young woman said doggedly.

"Maybe," Fargo allowed. "No clear footprints around to pin that down one way or the other."

"What are you saying? What do you think happened here?" Annabel questioned.

"Got no answers for that," he said. "But something different. I'll bet on that. Maybe the child will tell you."

"Yes," the girl said. "Let's get back to town and find out."

2

"This child won't be telling you anything today," the doctor said. "Her temperature was below normal when you brought her in. We've managed to bring that up and we got some soup into her. She's resting now."

"When will she be able to talk to us?" Annabel asked.

Fargo, standing at the back of the room, watched the doctor's lips draw back.

"I don't know. Maybe not for a long time. Maybe never," Doc Kerr said.

"Never?" The young woman frowned.

"She's in deep, deep shock. I've seen a case like this before. I'm thinking we can treat her body but not her mind. We can heal the flesh but not the soul," the doctor said solemnly.

"Are you saying she might never come around to talking?" Annabel pressed.

"She might. Something might reach her. But I don't know what or how. Maybe time will do it," the doctor said. "We'll just have to treat her gently and wait and see."

"I'm sure you'll do your best," the young woman said. She turned and walked from the doctor's office, the two men following her.

Fargo stepped out and saw her hurry away, the two

men still following. Fargo turned away and felt surprise poke at him. He'd expected something more from the girl—a few words, at least. But she was plainly in a hurry to be on her way. He shrugged and took the Ovaro's reins in one hand. He had his own things to do here in Mountainville.

He led the horse behind him as he walked down the single street of the town. Mountainville wasn't much of a town, he noted, even measured against other small western towns. He saw a small fur-trading outlet, a few grain sheds but no general store, no bank, no town hall, no schoolhouse, not even a barbershop. The saloon, marked by its swinging double doors and murmur of voices drifting out from inside, didn't even carry a name. But he spotted a two-story, gray-white house with a sign in front of it that read: TRAVELER'S ROOM & BOARD.

He stopped there, dropped the pinto's reins over the outside rail, and went in. A man with heavy spectacles and a green wool shirt looked up from behind a small desk. A bland-faced man with a noticeable paunch, he half-rose, then sank back into his chair. "Welcome, stranger. Want a room?" he asked.

"Want some information," Fargo said. "I thought this might be the place to get it. Or maybe you can point me to the mail depot or the sheriff's office."

"The mail drop's here and we don't have a sheriff in Mountainville," the man said. Fargo's eyebrows lifted. "We have a mayor and an undertaker. They sort of see to whatever's needed."

Fargo fished the letter from his pocket. "I'm looking to find an outfit called Dorrance and Company Enterprises," he said.

The man nodded. "They set up what you could call an office in the old cow barn at the end of town."

Fargo frowned at the answer. "That the way of things around here?"

"Sometimes."

"What keeps this town going?" Fargo queried with honest curiosity.

"We get enough wagon trains passing through on their way into Canada, especially those who want to follow the Kootenay River up. They make this a stop on their way. In winter we get enough folks who come down from the mountains to stay until the spring thaws," the man said.

"Much obliged." Fargo nodded. "I might just be back for that room." He turned and walked from the inn, staying on foot as he moved past the remaining buildings of the town and finally spotted the unmistakable structure of the old cow barn with its long body and high, small windows. The front door hung open and he halted before the piece of paper tacked to the outside wall with the name DORRANCE & COMPANY ENTERPRISES handwritten on it. A frown slid across his forehead as he entered the old barn. It deepened when he saw the lone table and the three straight-backed wood chairs inside the cavernous emptiness of the barn. Two of the three chairs were occupied, one by the apple-cheeked young woman, the other by her friend David Corry. Fargo knew surprise glinted in his eyes as he stared at them. "It seems we keep meeting," he said. "What brings you here?"

"I've been waiting," she said. "For you, actually."

"I'm looking for Dorrance and Company," Fargo said.

"I'm Annabel Dorrance."

"And Company?" Fargo frowned.

David Corry's voice cut in. "I'm the company part."

"Please sit down," Annabel said. She offered a smile.

Fargo didn't return it as he lowered himself onto the third chair. "What the hell is this all about?" he growled.

"I'm the one that wrote and hired you," she said.

"Why didn't you tell me that when we met before?" Fargo asked sharply.

"It didn't seem the right moment. I knew there'd be questions and explaining," Annabel said. She was working hard at maintaining an air of casual calm.

"You're goddamn right about that," he snapped, and shot a glance at the older man. David Corry's professorial face held uncomfortableness in it. "Your letter said Dorrance Enterprises," Fargo pressed, returning his eyes to the young woman. "Tell me about the enterprises."

She tried a quick smile. "This is the first one, really," she said.

"Wait a damn second," Fargo said. "Dorrance and Company is you and him, and there haven't been any damn enterprises?"

"Everyone has to start someplace," she said, summoning up a touch of righteousness.

"Not by making themselves out as a real and proper operation," Fargo cut in.

"This is just that. We are going into the Cabinet Mountains to set up a wildlife study center," the girl said.

"A what?" Fargo bit out.

"A place where we can study and record all the wildlife in this untamed region before people come in to change it," she said. "David, here, is a writer and teacher on mammals. I draw and paint."

Fargo felt his frown digging down over his eyes. "You two are going to set up shop in these mountains?"

"James Audubon did it, going around on his own," she snapped. "David did some work with Audubon many years ago."

"Audubon spent years getting to know the wild, how to live, how to survive, and he had experienced guides. He wasn't a damn apple-cheeked girl too young to know much of anything," Fargo tossed out.

Annabel's hazel eyes flared. "I know more than enough. Besides, we've gathered an entire troupe for our wildlife study center," Annabel returned. "We have Humphrey Asgood, an ornithologist, Avery Hodges who specializes in reptiles, Thomas Turner who studies insect life. That's five of us at the core of it. Then there'll be the others in the community."

"Community?" Fargo echoed.

"Yes," she snapped. "Our studies will take our full time. We can't be spending time on housework, building homes, food gathering, cooking, and all the other time-consuming things required to live. So I gathered together a group of people, settlers, who will be part of the entire project. They'll build the community, claim the land for their own, do everything that needs doing while we work, and they'll be paid for it in money as well as having the land for themselves when the rest of us leave. I'm bringing along a sizable amount of money to pay them as well as any other expenses that might come up."

"You're going up into the Cabinet Mountains and set up shop," Fargo said again. He felt the sense of amazement spinning inside himself.

"Exactly," she said.

"And these settlers, are they experienced people?"

"They're people who want a new chance at life," she answered.

"Where'd you find them?" Fargo asked.

"I advertised in newspapers back in Minnesota and farther east and in Kansas. I picked those who seemed anxious and stable, mostly good family people," Annabel said.

"With kids, of course," Fargo slid at her.

"Some," she said.

Fargo looked at David Corry and saw the older man sitting with a studious, attentive air. "You see it as a kind of big, outdoor classroom, I take it," Fargo said.

"Yes, that's putting it quite well." The man smiled.

Fargo shook his head in wonder. "I don't believe what I'm hearing," he said. "How many, not counting kids?"

"We five and about fifteen others. Twenty altogether," she said.

"Half women who've never pulled a trigger," Fargo grunted.

"There'll be ten experienced gunmen coming along," Annabel said, and his eyes questioned. "I hired them strictly as guards, outriders, protection. I hired them after I got here, men who were here in Mountainville. Now, have you heard enough?"

"I sure have, honey," Fargo said, and rose to his feet. "Good luck and good-bye," he tossed back as he strode from the old barn.

She came running from the open doorway as he swung onto the saddle, her breasts bouncing. "What's the matter with you? What are you doing?" she called out.

"I don't hanker to be a part of a pack of damn

fools," Fargo said, and sent the Ovaro into a fast trot.

He ignored her shouts and rode from town, staying on the path until he spotted a hillside of good bluegrass. He rode up it and let the Ovaro enjoy the softness underfoot. At the top of the hill he found a bower of mountain ash and slid to the ground. He settled himself against a tree while the horse wandered across the bluegrass to munch happily on the sweet, cool feed.

Resentment festered inside the Trailsman. He never liked being sold a bill of goods and he didn't like wild-goose chases, and this was both. Perhaps most of all, he could have been breaking trail for Jim Heller down Nevada way. But he'd turned Jim down because he'd obligated himself by accepting Annabel's letter and the advance money.

His eyes narrowed as he peered up into the high hills where he'd found the wagon and the little girl. The sound of a horse's hooves interrupted his thoughts. He looked down the hillside and saw the girl riding fast toward him. He stayed against the tree and watched her reach the arbor and swing to the ground. Her apple-cheeked face was clouded with fury.

"You can't do this," Annabel Dorrance flung at him. "You can't ride off and leave us. We've been waiting for you. You made an agreement."

"Not for this, honey," Fargo said. "You did a job on me with that letter. Or maybe you've a bad memory." He reached into his pocket, unfolded the square of paper, and began to read from it. " 'Because we have learned that you are the very best, Dorrance and Company Enterprises wants to hire you to break trail for our latest operation.' " He halted and threw a glare at her. " 'Dorrance and

Company have planned in detail. If you accept, let us know by return post and keep the money enclosed as payment to seal our agreement.' " He put down the letter and met her eyes. "Dorrance and Company Enterprises want you for our latest operation. Dorrance and Company have planned in detail," he repeated sarcastically. "Now, I'd say that sounds like a lot more than a collection of dreamers and damn fools."

"All right, perhaps you were misled somewhat by my letter," she sniffed.

"Misled!" Fargo snapped. "Try lied to."

She let herself look aloof. "I decided it would have been too involved to explain it all by letter."

"You knew I wouldn't take you on if you told me the truth of it by letter," Fargo threw back, and saw her full lips tighten.

"That's a matter of argument. The fact is you accepted, took the advance money, and came. That's an agreement and you can't toss it aside now. Besides, I didn't think you were the kind who broke agreements."

He found himself almost admiring the way she dismissed her own deceits and hurled accusations. "Good try, honey," he said, and she turned away to stare down the hillside. He leaned to the left to see her fighting back tears, and he felt a stab of surprise.

"You know Jed Backman," she murmured.

"I sure do," Fargo said. Jed was an old friend and a good man. "He never put you up to this."

"No, but he told me we'd no chance without you. That's why I wrote that letter the way I did. I knew I had to get to you."

Fargo drew a deep sigh. "Annabel, honey, you've no chance with me or without me," he said. "The

Cabinet Mountains are no place to set up a community. You need flatland to farm and graze cattle."

"Not always. Farmers in the Swiss Alps have been raising cattle on mountainsides for centuries," she returned.

He found himself smiling reluctantly. She had a fast mind and knew how to fight for herself. "Different kind of mountains, different kind of dangers, different kind of cattle," he said almost gently.

She blinked and he saw her fight back tears again. "Dammit, Fargo, Jed Backman said only you could find us a place where we'd have a chance. I've counted on you and you made an agreement. That's still a fact."

He watched her summon up anger to fill the hazel eyes. She had hold of some truth, he knew and he'd come to realize something else: She wasn't pleading out of pure damn-fool obstinacy. She was fighting for a dream, a vision she'd taken a lot of pain and effort to try to organize into a reality. For good or bad, she believed, she pursued a dream.

"Babes in the woods," he said with bitterness. "But I'll help you, on my conditions."

Her full lips parted and she all but flew at him as her arms circled his neck and she buried her face into his chest. He felt the warm, curving contours of her, breasts very soft against him. "Thank you, Fargo, oh, thank you," she murmured, and pulled back at once and he saw the color flood her apple cheeks. "I'm sorry," she said.

"Best thing you've done so far." He smiled, and then his eyes grew stern again. "My conditions, remember," he said.

"Which are?" she asked with caution in her voice.

"I call the shots, no matter how much its hurts."

28

"All right," Annabel agreed. "But you still don't think it can work."

"That's right."

"Having confidence, believing, that's important."

"That's your department, honey," Fargo said grimly.

"Why don't you think we can do it?" she asked.

"The mountains, the winters, the Nez Percé, the Northern Shoshoni, the Bannock, the mix of people you've put together, and every other hardship that'll come along," Fargo said.

"I'll have you meet everyone else tomorrow before we start. Maybe you'll change your mind," Annabel said.

"Wouldn't bet on it," Fargo grunted. He watched her walk away and swing onto the horse, her body a thing of graceful curves.

"Are you riding back to town with me?" she asked, all of her sweetness returned to give her an appealing vulnerability.

"No," he said. "Where do I find you in the morning?"

"Let's meet at the old barn," she said.

"Dorrance Enterprises' fancy office?" he slid at her, and received a quick flash of hazel fire.

"Very funny," she sniffed. "There's a waiting area a half-mile west of town. The others are there. I'll take you."

"Good enough." Fargo watched her ride down the hill, her brown hair flowing in thick folds as the wind caught at it.

He waited till she was out of sight before he pulled himself onto the Ovaro and slowly started up into the high hills. He rode slowly and finally found himself at the grisly scene once again, drawn there by reasons he could not give form to yet. He dismounted, fought away the sickening odor of decay and death, and carefully made his way across the gruesomeness of it. Once again, his keen, practiced eyes sought out details, all the tiny things that were so important but that most people passed over. He made his way through the brush surrounding the area, a frown on his brow. Finally he returned to the side of the overturned wagon, examined the remains of clothing, the still-closed wooden chests, the epitaphs of ordinariness that were perhaps peculiarly appropriate.

At last he turned away and remounted the pinto, his eyes hardened in thought as they swept the scene one more time. "Strange," he murmured aloud. "Very damn strange."

He turned the pinto away and slowly rode down through the high hills. He'd never been one for believing in omens or ill winds, but he very much believed that in the dark heart of the wild forest depths there lived evils and wisdoms beyond the knowing of mere humans.

===== 3 =====

Fargo woke early but allowed himself the luxury of another hour in the bed. He had decided to indulge himself and had returned to the inn during the night. Now, as the sun grew bolder in the room, he rose, washed, and dressed. He took a cup of coffee offered him from a cart in the lobby downstairs, let the bracing brew finish waking him, and finally rode the Ovaro down the main street of Mountainville to the old cow barn at the far end of town.

He felt his brow furrow when he neared the barn, angry voices coming from inside the open door, Annabel's first. "Get out. Leave me alone. You'd no right following me here," Fargo heard the young woman shout.

The man's voice shouted back at once, bitter anger in it. "Hell I didn't. You're not going to do this, dammit," he said.

"You've no right to interfere in my life, Barrat. Now, you get out of here," Annabel said.

Fargo halted and swung from the saddle just as David Corry's voice joined in, his tone calm and soothing.

"Annabel has asked you to leave. Be a gentleman and do so," Corry said.

"You threatening me, mister?" the first man's voice snapped harshly.

"No, I'm saying that Annabel has a right to make her own decision," Fargo heard Corry answer, his voice still calm. But the other man's voice was neither calm nor controlled.

"And I've a right to shut your face," the man said, and the sound of the blow followed, sharply and unexpectedly.

"Barrat!" Annabel Dorrance screamed.

With one long stride, Fargo was at the doorway and stepping inside the old barn. David Corry lay on the floor, shaking his head dazedly, and Fargo saw a tall, young man with long, straight black hair holding on to the young woman's wrist.

"No, damn you, let me go," Annabel screamed as she tried to twist away.

"You heard the lady," Fargo said quietly.

The man half-spun to face him but kept his grip on the girl's wrist. He had a tightly wound face, its handsomeness marred by the tense nervousness that was a part of its black eyes and thin lips.

"Get out of here, mister," the man she'd called Barrat ordered.

"Fargo, please help me," Annabel said. Suddenly, she managed to tear herself away from the man's grip.

"Fargo?" Barrat said. "I heard you'd arrived. Now you can leave."

David Corry had shaken away his daze and began to push himself to his feet, Fargo saw as his eyes went to Annabel. "What the hell is all this about?" he asked.

"His name's Barrat Dowling and he's crazy," Annabel said.

Fargo's eyes went to the young man who took a step toward him.

"You're cutting out, Fargo, here and now," Dowling growled.

"Why?" Fargo asked, curiosity prodding him.

"Because without you she can't do it. Without you, it all falls apart," Dowling said. "I heard about you. That's why I came."

"She can go on without me," Fargo said. "She probably would."

"No, it's all done with without you," Dowling repeated, his young, tight face sneering with its own tensions.

"Maybe, but that's not for you to decide, sonny," Fargo said calmly.

The man's face darkened with instant fury. "You high tail it, dammit, or what happened to him will be nothing compared to what I'll do to you," he said, indicating David Corry.

"I do believe Annabel is right about you, sonny. You're plumb loco," Fargo said. He saw the younger man's brow lower, his shoulders drop. The Trailsman was ready for the looping blow that sailed at him. He twisted to the side and the blow almost grazed his jaw, Barrat Dowling's arms a fraction longer than he had guessed. The man tried to follow through with a roundhouse right, but Fargo brought up a whistling uppercut. It caught Dowling under the point of his chin and he staggered backward for a few steps before he went down. Fargo took a step toward him, but he saw the younger man roll and come up on his feet, his tight, tense face twisted with fury.

Dowling fired two lightening-quick left jabs that Fargo barely managed to avoid, then a third that Fargo parried. The man had fast hands, Fargo saw, his own eyes narrowed as he parried another two blows—one a left hook, the other a looping right.

Dowling returned to his quick jabs again and Fargo gave ground. The younger man leapt with boldness and bored forward with confidence, a half-sneering grin stretching his lips. He shot a left hook that Fargo let graze his cheek as he twisted away, followed with another fast jab. Fargo, in a crouch, took the jab alongside the temple and, with all the power of his muscled shoulders, smashed a straight left upward. It landed flush on Dowling's jaw and the man stopped in his tracks as his head snapped back. He blinked and never saw the right cross that followed, but the blow lifted him from his feet and he flew backward. He crashed into the edge of one of the old stalls and the wood splintered as he slowly sank to the floor.

Fargo brought his eyes up to Annabel Dorrance. "You want to tell me about him?" he said grimly.

"Yes, of course," she said. Fargo saw Corry continue to dab at blood from his lip as he uttered a sigh of relief. "I'm terribly sorry about this, Fargo . . ." the young woman began.

Fargo had picked up the sound and turned from her to see Dowling had regained consciousness with the resiliency of youth. He watched the man push himself to his feet, hate blazing in his black eyes. He was the kind who had to save face, Fargo knew, and he had already anticipated the man's next move and was prepared for it. When Barrat Dowling went for his gun, Fargo had the Colt in his hand in one instant motion and he fired before Dowling's six gun cleared its holster.

"Jesus," Dowling screamed in pain as the gun flew from his fingers and he clutched at his hand. He half-turned away, turned back, and stared at the big Colt trained on him.

"That could've been between your eyes, sonny," Fargo said. "The next one will be, if you try that again." He holstered the Colt and watched the young man back from the barn, halt to carefully pick up his gun while still clutching his fingers with his other hand. "Don't come back," Fargo said with quiet firmness.

Barrat Dowling paused in the doorway. "She can't do it without you," he snarled. "You're not taking her damn wagons, Fargo. You're not taking her anyplace." He spun on his heel and a moment later Fargo saw him atop a horse as he raced away.

The Trailsman turned back to Annabel. "You were saying?" he remarked, dropping the Colt back into its holster casually.

"Let's ride while we talk," she said, and he shrugged agreement.

"We all owe you a vote of thanks, Fargo," Corry said. "That's obviously a very disturbed young man."

Fargo said nothing but watched Annabel as she climbed onto a sturdy brown with a white streak down its foreface. She wore a deep-tan blouse that lay against the lovely curve of her breasts and she held herself very straight in the saddle, he noted. Fargo swung onto the Ovaro and saw David Corry mount a small horse and tag along behind.

"Barrat Dowling was a boyfriend once, I take it," Fargo said.

"No," she said, snapping the word out in anger. "Not really." He questioned with his glance and she went on. "I saw him for a short while and then broke it off, but he never believed I meant it. He made our relationship into something it never was, all inside his head. He kept seeing us as lovers."

"Were you ever?" Fargo questioned.

"No, not ever. There was an occasional kiss but never anything more. But he saw it all differently in his mind. He's crazy, Fargo. I suspected as much then. That's why I broke up with him. He frightened me then and he does now."

"And he followed you all the way here," Fargo said.

"He told me he would, but I didn't believe him," Annabel said with a toss of her gold-brown hair. She drew a sigh from deep inside herself. "Perhaps you scared him off once and for all."

"Not likely," Fargo said, and she peered back. "A man with that kind of twisted pain doesn't back off. It cuts too deep."

"I'm not afraid now that you're here," she said.

His quick glance told him the reply was no attempt at glib flattery. "Keep being afraid," he said. "Fear is better than overconfidence."

Annabel half-smiled and put her horse into a trot. "Let's go meet the others," she said, and Fargo swung in beside her.

They had ridden a few hundred yards when the three wagons crossed in front of them and Annabel slowed to a halt. The man driving the first wagon, a woman beside him, waved at her.

"The Hostler wagons," she said in an aside to Fargo. "That's Sam Hostler. They'd have joined with us, but we'll be searching for the right place while they're going straight across the mountains."

Fargo frowned at the man on the wagon. "Never heard of a trail across the mountains," he said.

"We've a map that shows it," the man said. "A prospector sold it to us. It's marked real clear and puts us all the way across and into Bonners Ferry in Idaho Territory."

"Good luck," Fargo said, and with another wave the man led his three wagons and Fargo felt Annabel's eyes on him.

"Spit it out," she said.

"More damn fools," he grunted. "There's no such trail across the mountains. Somebody sold him a map with a trapper's trail you can't drive a toy wagon through."

"Maybe we'll catch up to them after a while," Annabel said. "I'll talk some more to Sam Hostler." She moved forward and soon Fargo saw the half-circle of wagons come into sight in a clearing of land. He reined to a halt and dismounted as Annabel swung from her horse. Though figures hurried from the wagons to gather in front of him, his eyes swept past them to travel across the wagons. Most, he was glad to see, were California rack beds, mountain wagons with fifty-two-inch wheels and outfitted with canvas tops. One was a Baker's wagon, painted green with sliding side doors and drop windows that were properly curtained, rigged out with a one-horse drive shaft. No cumbersome Conestogas, he saw gratefully.

Annabel led him to three men standing with David Corry. They varied in height and weight and facial features, but all wore the same, slightly abstract, studious air as David Corry. "Humphrey Asgood, ornithology," Annabel introduced. Fargo nodded to the man and followed Annabel. "Avery Hodges, serpents," she said, "and Thomas Turner, insects."

After brief handshakes, Fargo went with her as she moved along the line of people in front of their wagons. He took in solid family types, most in their early thirties, a handful of youngsters standing by. Fargo tried to fasten their names in his mind as Annabel introduced them but knew he'd have to learn them over again in time.

A beefy, black-haired man stepped forward and spoke to Annabel with apology in his voice. "Got a broken rear axle, Miss Annabel. It'll take three days most likely before it's fixed enough to roll. You can start on and we'll try to catch up. I know delays are no good."

Annabel glanced at Fargo and read his gaze. "No, we'll wait, Harding," she said. "It's best we stay together." The fifth wagon was next and Fargo took in a man perhaps fifty years of age but still burly, with black hair and eyes to match set in a stern, dour face that, he was sure, seldom smiled. The woman beside him, at least twenty-five years younger, wore a long gray dress with a square-cut neckline. Heavy, deep breasts pushed up out of the top of the neckline. She had a broad attractive face with full lips, a slightly flat nose, and dark eyes that smoldered as they met his gaze. "Herb and Vivian Starr," Annabel said. "Herb's a carpenter. We're counting on his knowledge to help us build our cabins."

The man nodded and even that seemed an effort, his dour expression unchanged. But the woman stepped forward with a warm smile. "I've heard about you, Fargo. I feel better with you here," she said.

"That's good." Fargo smiled back. He noticed Herb Starr watching with his dour, stern expression. The smile left Vivian Starr's lips but continued to dance in her dark eyes as she stepped back.

"This is my wagon," Annabel said, and halted before the converted Baker's wagon. She pulled the back door open and let him see a mattress that took up one side of the wagon with boxes and clothes neatly arranged along the other side. He bent low to peer at the undercarriage. it was light yet sturdy enough to hold up, he decided. "You'll be lead wagon," he said, straightening up.

"I expected that," Annabel said sharply.

"For now," Fargo said, and met her eyes.

"I'm sorry about the delay, but perhaps you'll enjoy a few days' rest," she said.

"I'll try," Fargo said.

"Change your mind about our chances, now that you've met most of us?" she asked.

"Nope," he said. She hesitated and whatever she was about to answer was cut off as the group of horsemen came into sight and rode to a halt. "Your protection?" Fargo said, and she nodded. He watched the leading rider dismount and walk toward her.

"This is Dick Terrall," Annabel introduced. The man nodded. Fargo saw a cruel mouth and one eye that twitched in a lined, heavy face. Terrall sported a slight paunch on a powerful frame and had eyes that appraised Fargo with icy hardness.

"So you're Fargo, the famous Trailsman," Terrall said, and made no attempt to disguise the sneer in his voice. "I hope you're worth whatever she's payin' you."

"Guess we'll find that out," Fargo answered calmly.

"We sure will," Terrall said. Disdain was plain in his attitude. "Only I don't have to wait for that answer," he added, ending the sentence with a derisive snort.

Fargo's eyes went past the man and he felt the grimness curl inside him. Terrall was accompanied by a collection of small-time gunhands, scroungers and two-bit drifters who had lived crafty lives, more often than not on the wrong side of the law. It was in their jaundiced eyes, the bitterness of their mouths, the scruffiness of their chaps, and the worn leather of holsters never saddle-soaped properly. He brought his eyes back to Terrall. The man's dislike was almost palpable. Annabel may have bought herself more trouble than protection, Fargo decided. He turned away from the man.

"There's been a delay," he heard Annabel said. "We mightn't leave for two days, but you'd best check in every morning."

"Whatever you say, boss lady." Terrall turned away, climbed on his horse, and led his men away.

Fargo watched them go until they were out of sight. When he turned, he saw Annabel's eyes on him.

"I didn't hire them for their character," she said. "And he resents you being here. He said he could break trail for us. I think it's a matter of simple jealousy."

"Do you, now?" Fargo half-smiled.

"That's right. As I said, I hired them for their guns, not their character."

"They don't always stay separate," Fargo muttered.

"They've no reason to come along except for pay," Annabel said.

"Didn't you say you were bringing along a fair sum of money for payment to your settler families and for expenses?" Fargo reminded her. She frowned at him. "Money draws takers the way honey draws flies."

"What a terrible thing to say. That would make them out-and-out bandits," she said, and drew herself together. "No, I won't believe that. No." She stopped, frowned at him. "You've no right making that kind of accusation based only on your own suspicious nature."

"I didn't do any accusing, honey. I just pointed out possibilities."

"Which are always negative with you."

"Not always." Fargo smiled and found himself thinking of Vivian Starr's eyes, which could dance and smolder at the same time.

A gray-haired figured approached, rounded, with pale cheeks given a little color by the red shirt he wore. Humphrey Asgood, the bird expert, Fargo remembered.

"Annabel, my dear." the man said excitedly. "I came upon a perfect specimen of wood lily just back of the camp. You ought to take these extra few days to get it down on paper."

"I will, Humphrey," Annabel said, and cast a glance at Fargo. "You're welcome to take supper with us tonight, Fargo," she said. "Six o'clock."

"I just might," Fargo nodded and walked away, the pinto following him. He climbed into the saddle a dozen yards on and took the horse up into the low foothills, where he rode in a slow path along the bottom of the hills, his eyes searching out openings in the forest land. He found one that would do to start the wagons upward and he followed it into the low hills. There he found a ledge and stared out at the dense mountain forests. Beauty and ugliness lived in those forests, good and evil hid in those dark-green depths, life and death waited side by side. There were the dangers a man could know and guard against, and there were the unknown ones. And a scene of strange carnage came into his thoughts, perhaps something darker.

The feeling persisted, much as he tried to shake it away, and he was glad to turn the Ovaro downhill as dusk began to slide across the low hills.

It was dark when he returned to the half-circle of wagons, and the odor of roast pork stirred the appetite. He took a plate offered by one of the women and sat down by himself. Annabel engaged in animated conversation with the four other naturalists and nodded to him, then he saw the full-length gray dress appear at his side. Vivian Starr folded herself down beside him and her smoldering brown eyes regarded him with private amusement.

"You wouldn't remember me, of course," she said.

"Am I supposed to?" Fargo asked.

"No, but I was in Hoot Falls a few years ago. Mary McKay introduced me to you," Vivian Starr said with a silent laugh in her voice, and Fargo felt his own smile come to his lips. Memory washed over him, all of it pleasant. Mary McKay had been a happy interlude he well remembered. "Mary told me you were something special," the woman said.

"You hankering to find out for yourself?" he slid at her. The question didn't bother her, he saw, as she smiled, her broad face attractive in the firelight.

"Maybe, but I've something more on my mind," she said, suddenly growing serious. "I can't talk now. I'll find a time and place. Just expect me."

Fargo nodded and she rose and left to turn in her plate. His slow glance around the camp caught Herb Starr's dour face watching his wife with his eyes narrowed. Fargo also took note of something else as Annabel sauntered over to him.

"Vivian Starr seems quite friendly with you," Annabel said with only a thin veil of disapproval in her voice.

"Nothing wrong with being friendly," Fargo said.

"No, of course not," she retreated a little.

"Terrall and his men don't take meals with you, it appears," Fargo remarked.

"No, they stay pretty much by themselves," Annabel said. "That's their privilege. It doesn't mean anything."

"Guess not," Fargo said, and drew a cool glance from the girl. "See you sometime tomorrow," he said as he rose and handed in his plate. He walked to the Ovaro and climbed onto the horse to make his way from the camp, aware of Annabel's eyes following him until he melted into the night. He rode slowly and let thoughts revolve through his mind. Barrat Dowling wasn't about to go away. The question was whether he was really a danger. Maybe Dick Terrall was more of a danger. Fargo tossed the questions as he rode, and knew one thing above all else: he never liked waiting around to be a target. Maybe he could give them both a chance to tip their hands. It was worth a try, he decided, and when he reached Mountainville, he halted outside the saloon.

The hum of voices drifted through the swinging door. He dismounted and went into the smoky air of the room. A long bar took up most of one side and his eyes swept across the men drinking there, coming to a halt at the tall figure with the long, straight black hair at the far end of the bar.

Barrat Dowling's tightly handsome face turned and saw him, and Fargo saw the tension flood the man's face at once. Barrat watched him go to the bar and order a bourbon before he gulped down his drink and almost rushed from the saloon. It was as if he'd been upset at being seen.

Fargo frowned and turned his eyes on the tables as he sipped the bourbon. He paused when he saw Terrall and four of his men at a corner table. The other five were seated at the next table. Terrall watched him at the bar but made no sign of recognition, so Fargo turned his attention to the bourbon, savoring it in small sips. He was pleasantly surprised to find it better bourbon than he'd expected in this out-of-the-way hole.

He nursed the drink, let the hours slip by, finally ordered another, and watched the saloon begin to empty. Without girls or entertainment, the Mountainville saloon was plainly not a place for late-night drinking. There were perhaps only a dozen men left in the saloon when Fargo finished the last of the bourbon and casually scanned the room. Terrall was still there, along with those at his table. But two of the men at the adjoining table had quietly left.

A grim smile flicked across Fargo's lips as he set the glass down. He strolled across the room and went out into the dark night, pausing to scan the silent street and the handful of buildings. If a surprise party was planned for him, it was likely they'd wait till he left town, yet he couldn't be sure. He unhitched the pinto and led the horse down a side alley where he halted and took his bedroll out, propped it up vertically on the saddle, and tied it in place with a length of lariat.

He took his jacket off, draped it over the bedroll, put his hat on top, stepped back, and was satisfied with the hasty dummy. The night was almost moonless, he noted gratefully, a sliver of a new moon peeking through fast-moving clouds. He sent the Ovaro out onto the street, and staying hard against the building line, where the shadows were deepest, he kept pace with the horse as the pinto slowly moved up the still street. The Ovaro reached the end of town and Fargo, in a crouch, ran to the horse in a half-dozen long strides. He pointed the pinto along the narrow road that led out of town, slapped the horse smartly on the rump, and watched him trot off along the road. The Trailsman darted back into the trees that lined the road and broke into his own loping trot that kept him not more than a dozen paces behind the pinto. Fargo moved through the trees, one eye on the horse as he trotted along the road. Eventually the Ovaro began to slow down of his own accord.

The horse trotted on another hundred yards, slowing to a walk where the trees on both sides of the road leaned in. Fargo was moving closer when the two shots split the night. He dropped to one knee and saw the Ovaro halt, then kick up his heels as the bullets smashed into the object on his back. The figure on the horse appeared to fall sideways from the saddle as the shots struck it. The horse pawed the ground, alarmed and uncertain. The figure seemed to hang from the saddle. The big Colt in his hand, Fargo saw the two riders come out of the trees and race toward the Ovaro. The Trailsman began to run and reached the edge of the road just as the two men pulled to a halt beside the Ovaro.

"What the hell?" he heard one snort.

"Surprise, gents," Fargo said as he crouched. "Don't move."

But the two men wheeled their horses around to face him and Fargo saw both go for their guns. He fired and one toppled from his horse. The second man ducked low in the saddle, firing off a wild shot as he sent his mount into a gallop. Fargo rose and raced for the Ovaro, vaulted onto the horse, and pulled the bedroll up across the saddle in front of him as he sent the pinto forward. The second man had turned into the trees, his sound easy to follow as he raced in headlong flight.

Fargo closed ground quickly. He caught sight of the dark shape ahead of him as the man was forced to slow to skirt the trees where the forest grew thicker. Suddenly the fleeing figure reined up, turned, and fired a volley of shots at his pursuer. Fargo flattened himself on the Ovaro and heard the bullets slam wildly into the trees around him. He didn't slow the Ovaro's pace and saw the man turn and start to race on again.

Fargo spurred the Ovaro through a cluster of cottonwoods, and racing almost parallel to the other horse, he drew the Colt. He wanted the man alive to answer questions, especially if he'd been hired by Barrat Dowling, but the night blackness, the trees, and his erratic pace made accuracy all but impossible. Fargo brought the Colt up, pressed the trigger, and saw his shot miss the man's black bulk by a fraction of an inch. But the man yanked his horse hard in an attempt to make a sharp swerve. The horse lost its balance, slamming hard against the side of a tree. The man's figure went backward over the horse's rump and Fargo heard the short, guttural cry of pain that ended as quickly as it had begun. He slowed the Ovaro, turned, and made for the figure on the ground, cursing silently as he reined to a halt and jumped to the ground. He knelt down and saw the branch protruding from the man's neck. The horse had slammed him into a low length of branch with full force when it crashed into the tree. He'd answer no questions on anything, Fargo realized, but he recognized the man as one of Terrall's band by his long jaw and light-brown mustache.

Fargo pushed to his feet, emitted a long sigh, and returned to the Ovaro. He rode slowly back through the forest, emerged onto a slow slope, and took it until he found a spot to bed down. He laid out his bedroll and was grateful to see that the two shots had gone only through the top edge. He undressed in the warm night and stretched out as thoughts floated through his mind. He knew two things for certain about Terrall: the man had a lot more than jealousy and resentment inside him; he wanted no one around who could give him problems. And now that he had tried and failed, he'd have to try again.

But not right away. He'd wait for a better opportunity next time. Fargo's eyes narrowed in thought. Terrall would be one of the dangers to guard against, but somehow, he kept feeling that the real dangers to come were still shrouded in the dark-green depths of the wild.

He closed his eyes and let the warm night wind pull sleep over him.

===== 4 =====

The morning sun sifted its way through the trees as he slowly rode through the wood behind the wagons until he found her, seated on a stump with a shaft of light beaming down on her. It gave the gold-brown hair added glints of copper, and he saw she had a small square of canvas on her lap and a palette of colors at her side. The wood lily, a half-dozen feet away, glowed like a flaming orange-red torch in the dark green of the forest. Annabel looked up as he came closer and climbed down from the horse to gaze at the canvas.

"I'm no art critic, but it seems to me you've set that wood lily down real fine," Fargo told her. "You're real good."

"Thank you." Annabel smiled and he watched her mix colors on a palette. She wore a loose, smocklike dress that revealed the soft-white edge of one breast every time she leaned over to the palette. "I'm really just about finished," she said finally, leaning back and taking a last narrow-eyed look at the flower and the painting on the canvas. Satisfied, she set the canvas down against the stump and began to clean the small palette with a jar of turpentine. "Harriet Crowler keeps a pot of coffee on all day. Will you come back with me and have a cup?" Annabel asked.

"Why not?" Fargo nodded.

"I've some good news. Harding says he'll be ready to roll come morning," she announced.

"I've some bad news," Fargo said. "You're going to have two less outriders." She frowned back. "Two of Terrall's men tried to bushwhack me last night. Their last mistake."

He watched the shocked disbelief flood her face. "No, that can't be," she said.

"A man knows when he's bushwhacked."

"Yes, but you're mistaken about who did it," she answered. "It wasn't any of Dick Terrall's men."

"They were Terrall's boys. I recognized one. Bushy, light-brown mustache," Fargo said. "You'll have eight riders now."

"No, I can't believe that. They were probably men Barrat Dowling hired. You heard him threaten you."

"Terrall's boys," Fargo repeated flatly as the wagons came into sight. He walked to her wagon where she carefully put away her canvas and paints. Then she led him to one of the other rigs where a tall, pleasant-faced woman stood by a coffee pot of gargantuan proportions. She handed Annabel a mug of the hot brew and another to him with a pleasant smile. He'd taken but a few sips when the band of riders approached, Terrall in the lead, and Fargo caught Annabel's quick, apprehensive glance at him. He took another sip of the coffee as Terrall brought his men to a halt in front of Annabel.

"We'll be pulling out tomorrow morning, bright and early," she said to him.

"Good. We'll be here," Terrall said. He brought his gaze up to Fargo. His heavy face stayed expressionless, his twitching eye the only movement in it, but there was boldness in his gaze.

Fargo kept his own expression bland and saw Annabel's eyes sweep the riders and she stepped back as Terrall turned and, with a wave, led his men from the campsite. She turned her hazel orbs on the big man alongside her, who continued to sip his coffee.

"Ten men," she said. "I counted ten men, not eight."

"So did I," Fargo said with a wry smile.

"You admit you were wrong, now?" she said.

"I wasn't wrong. He's clever. He made sure to get himself two replacements real fast instead of coming up with some explanation you mightn't buy," Fargo said.

"Can't you ever admit you made a mistake?" Annabel snapped.

"I can," Fargo said. "When I make one."

"You are an obstinate man." Annabel frowned.

"Especially when I'm right," Fargo agreed cheerfully. He drained the last of the coffee and returned the mug to Harriet Crowler. He climbed onto the pinto and slowly rode from the campsite, aware of Annabel's round-cheeked glower.

He turned the horse up into the nearby hills in the warm midday sun, found a flat place with some shade, and settled down to enjoy the scenery that stretched out in front of him. He hadn't settled for long when he spotted the lone horse and rider moving up the hillside, long brown hair flowing gently in a soft wind. The long gray dress had been changed to a brown riding skirt and a light-brown blouse. he watched Vivian Starr peer across the hillside, obviously searching for someone.

He rose to his feet and let her see him. She turned the horse toward him at once, and as she rode closer, his eyes scanned the hillside below, narrowed, and finally returned to the woman, who dismounted when she reached him. "Saw you ride up this way and decided to follow. I told you I wanted to talk," Vivian said.

"Sit down," Fargo offered, and she took his hand as she folded herself onto the soft fescue grass, holding on a few moments longer than necessary. She leaned back on her elbows, her breasts thrusting upward with a deep curve.

"I want out of this whole thing, Fargo," Vivian said. "Herb signed the contract to go on this with Annabel Dorrance. I was against it from the start."

"I can't see you can do much about it."

"Not right now, but you can help me."

"How?"

"I've some money of my own saved up. I'll pay you to get me out if anything goes wrong," she said.

"And the hell with the others?" Fargo smiled.

"Annabel and her group want to do this. So do most of the others. They made their beds. I didn't want any of it."

"Anything goes wrong, I'll do my best to help everyone. That'll include you, honey."

The woman looked out across the grass, her flat face glistening in the hot sun, an earthy attractiveness to her, the smoldering brown eyes darkly turbulent. "I figured you'd say something like that," she breathed. "Then I'll pay you to take me with you when you leave. You can do that."

Fargo let his lips pause. "Maybe," he said. "What about your husband?"

"The hell with him. I just want out of here before it all goes wrong."

"What makes you think it will?" Fargo queried.

"Something inside me. I've a feeling. I get these feelings, premonitions I heard them called," Vivian said, and her dark eyes turned to him. "They're almost always right. I'm scared, Fargo, real scared."

"You tell Herb about this?"

"He won't listen to me," Vivian said. "I suppose you're wondering about Herb and me."

"Some," Fargo admitted.

"Marrying Herb was a matter of convenience for both of us at the time. I was stranded. I'd a lot of debts because of a store I had that went broke. He needed somebody to look after his niece. It seemed an even exchange," Vivian Starr said, paused, and a wry smile touched her lips. "I even thought it would come to more in time."

"And it didn't?"

"Not the way I expected. Seems he'd been hurt years ago, a fall from a horse. He can't do a damn thing in bed and he won't do anything pleasurable for me. Then he started to keep a real tight rein on me so's I couldn't enjoy myself with anyone else. Life was hell, Fargo. When he finally sent the niece to a sister-in-law, I told him I wanted out. He laughed at me."

"You're telling me you're a kind of prisoner."

"That's a good way to put it," Vivian said with bitterness. "I tried to get away, with men I met who were willing to help me. They were both killed, shot in the back at night. Once I ran off on my own. He got a sheriff to bring me back as a runaway wife."

"Within his legal rights," Fargo grunted.

"Yes, the bastard. That's how he gets his kicks. Keeping me as a damn slave."

"What makes you think he won't come after you if you leave with me?"

"He'll have to stay here. He signed to do so, and he likes money too much to turn it down. I'll be far away by the time he tried to find me."

Fargo's half-smile was tinged with grimness.

"He's down near the bottom of the hill. I spotted him moving along behind you."

The woman's eyes took on a moment of surprise that quickly turned to anger. "That figures. I don't give a damn, and I know you can take care of yourself," she said.

"If I have to." Fargo shrugged. "We'll talk more about this, Vivian. There'll be time." He rose and pulled her to her feet, and her brown eyes were dark with seriousness.

"I hope so, Fargo. I'm scared. I keep feeling something real bad's going to happen. I keep seeing it inside me."

"What do you see, Vivian?" Fargo asked sharply. "Tell me what you see. Do you see arrows, an Indian attack? A mud slide? What do you see?"

"No, nothing like that, just all of us dead," she murmured, and her brown eyes were dark pools of turbulence that stared into space. She shook her head and brought herself back from the dark thoughts. "I'll be going now," she said, her voice suddenly tired.

He stepped back and watched her climb onto the horse and slowly move down the hillside. His gaze swept the trees at the bottom of the hill. Herb Starr hadn't reappeared. Perhaps he'd just stayed out of sight, perhaps he'd returned to the wagons. It didn't matter. He'd seen her come to meet him. The man could spell real trouble. But Fargo was more concerned over Vivian Starr's inner visions—those premonitions, as she'd called them. He'd heard of the likes of them before. They weren't always right, and often they were damn foolish. But now they confirmed his own suspicions. He'd not scoff.

He settled back down to take advantage of the warm, lazy time, and a smile edged his lips. Vivian

Starr had added a new dimension to the trip. And perhaps a new danger. He shrugged, lay back, and closed his eyes. Dangers known were better than those unknown.

He let the day dwindle down to dusk, and when he returned to the wagons, the odor of roasting chicken filled the air. He dismounted and walked to where Annabel, David Corry, and Avery Hodges, the snake naturalist, were fixing a canvas tie on one of the rigs. "I've a few questions before we roll in the morning," he said, and nodded to the very last rack bed. "That rig sits heavier than any of the others. Why?"

"That's our supply wagon. All our tools, all our extra equipment, everything is in that wagon, along with all our extra rifles and our ammunition," Avery Hodges said. "We are going to study nature, but we recognize the necessity of guns for food and protection."

"You better," Fargo grunted. "Why not spread your equipment over all the wagons, lighten the load on that one?"

"This way we know where everything is if we need something. We know exactly where to go. It's simpler and faster," Hodges answered.

"Maybe, but it's dangerous. You lose that wagon, you lose everything," Fargo pointed out.

"At least two of us will be with it at all times. We'll stay with it, ride with it, sleep in it. We realize how important it is to us," Hodges said.

Fargo half-shrugged as he turned away. "Your decision," he said, and took a plate of chicken and sat down alone to eat.

When he finished, he gathered up his bedroll and walked to the far edge of the campsite. Vivian Starr paused in taking garments down from a clothesline to send a smile his way, and he saw the silhouetted figure of her husband behind the canvas side of the wagon.

Fargo went into the first line of trees and found himself closest to Annabel's converted baker's wagon. He stretched out and the camp grew still. He was about to close his eyes when he saw the rear panel door of the wagon open and Annabel step out. She held a bucket of wash water and tossed it into the trees. Fargo saw the moonlight outline a deliciously curved figure under a diaphanous nightgown, full-cupped breasts turning up above a narrow waist and delightfully rounded hips. She returned to the wagon and pulled the door closed. Fargo lay back and let sleep come over him, anxious for the morning to arrive.

The night stayed quiet, and when morning came, he was washed and dressed and waiting as the others began to emerge from their wagons. He felt the excitement that gripped the camp. Avery Hodges and David Corry were busy as bees checking out every inch of their wagon. Annabel, in Levi's and a blue denim workshirt, nonetheless managed to look excitingly attractive. He watched her climb into the front of her baker's wagon and put down the drop windows. He saw her eyes on Dick Terrall as the man rode up with his crew.

"Where do you want us, Trailsman?" Terrall asked, the faint sneer part of his heavy face along with the eyes that twitched.

"Five on each side of the wagons. Keep generally abreast of the whole line," Fargo said. He saw that Terrall had decided to face him brazenly. But Fargo smiled inwardly as he suddenly realized that Terrall had no other choice. The man had no way of knowing whether his bushwhackers had been recognized.

It'd make him even more careful, Fargo knew as he turned the Ovaro and rode past Annabel. He halted, waved at her as he called out. "Move out," he said, and put the pinto into a trot. He hadn't gone far when he saw the lone horseman nearby, waiting and watching, and he sent the Ovaro toward the tense-faced, tall man with the long black hair and burning eyes.

"Don't get any ideas of riding along with us, Dowling," Fargo warned. "And don't get any ideas about anything else."

"It's a free country. I can ride wherever I damn well please," Barrat Dowling returned, his thin lips almost bloodless.

"Stay out of my sight," Fargo snapped. "I catch sight of you, I might blow your head off."

"You've no call to do that."

"I might mistake you for a Shoshoni," Fargo answered, watching the fury in Dowling's eyes.

"You're not taking her on this damn trip," Dowling threatened.

"I said my piece, sonny. Pay attention if you've any sense left." Fargo wheeled the Ovaro away and returned to the wagons. He waved them forward again, rode on, and put the pinto into a trot.

He rode through the low hills along a trail he found and paused from time to time to let the wagons catch sight of him and follow. Barrat Dowling had disappeared, but he wasn't gone, Fargo was certain. The man burned with a twisted possessiveness that made him dangerous. But to Annabel more than the wagons, Fargo reflected. He'd do in the wagons if he had the chance, but Dowling was more apt to make his direct move against Annabel. Fargo made a mental note to talk to the girl about that.

He made his way along the trail as it turned, growing narrower but remaining wide enough. The uphill climb didn't grow too steep, and when he came to a flat place that afforded a view of the terrain, he halted and his eyes swept the land on all sides.

Nothing moved. Barrat Dowling, somewhere in the deep green forest, remained carefully out of sight. Fargo moved on and it was midday when he reined up to stare down at a deep trench that cut across the trail. Perhaps six feet deep and at least ten feet wide, Fargo estimated, created by furious mountain rains and no doubt made deeper by each storm. He turned and rode to the right, then back to the left, but he saw the trench stretched with seeming endlessness. He returned to the trail as Annabel appeared with her wagon. She dismounted and gazed with dismay at the trench.

"There's no way around it," Fargo said.

"We can't go across it, not without wrecking every wagon," she murmured.

"We'll have to make it so we can cross," Fargo said. He swung from the saddle and saw the others had walked from their rigs to stare at the trench. "Start gathering branches, any kind of wood you can find. When you've finished with everything on the ground, start cutting down low branches."

"You're going to fill it," Annabel said, excitement catching her voice.

"Pack it with enough wood so the wagons can make it across," Fargo said. "Let's get started." He saw Annabel look at Dick Terrall and his men, who continued to stay on their horses.

"We hired on as guards, not woodchoppers," Terrall said gruffly.

"That's not a very good attitude," Annabel said, her jaw tightening.

"The man's right," Fargo cut in. "He'll stand

guard, on both sides of the road. You can't be too careful."

Terrall gave a snort of satisfaction and moved his men into the trees as Annabel began to gather wood alongside Fargo.

"You really expect trouble this far down in the low hills?" she questioned. "Did you see signs of Indians?"

"No," he answered, gathering an armful of wood from the forest floor.

"Then why'd you stop me from ordering Terrall to pitch in and help?" Annabel flared.

"It's important that Mr. Terrall feels confident," Fargo said, and drew a narrow-eyed stare from her.

"Don't play your little games at our expense, Fargo," she said. "We can use their help."

"I'm not playing games, honey," Fargo growled. "It's important for you as well as me."

"I don't understand."

"You will when the time comes," he told her. "Now just keep getting wood. He turned from her and brought his load back to the trench and watched the others scurry back and forth with wood—men, women, and some of the youngsters. But they were slowed when they had to begin cutting down low branches to fill the trench from side to side.

Fargo called a halt when night began to fall. "We'll finish in the morning," he said, and drew a grateful glance from Annabel. A supper of warm beef strips and johnnycakes was over quickly, everyone showing the weariness.

As Fargo put his bedroll down at the edge of the trees, he looked down the line of wagons. He saw Dick Terrall and his men settling down beyond the last wagon, keeping to themselves. He watched the men form two rows as they settled down. He lay back, closed his eyes, and slept at once.

He was up before the others when morning came, and stood at the edge of the trench with his eyes narrowed. They had half-filled the wide swatch of the gulley and he lowered himself down to the branches and walked across to the other side and back again. He looked up to see Annabel there and pulled himself out of the trench with his lips tight.

"Something wrong?" she asked.

"Too much give. We'll need twice as many branches," he said.

The others had begun to come up and turned away to begin dropping down more of the low branches. Fargo cast a glance at Terrall and saw he had his men casually lounging along the treeline, but he decided to say nothing. He took an ax Seth Crowler gave him and began to bring down the lower branches of the trees nearest him. He stopped counting after his tenth trip to the trench, but he finally halted and saw the branches piled over the edges of the trench.

"This ought to do it," he said, and motioned to Annabel. "Take your wagon over," he ordered, and stepped back as she climbed into the rig and began to roll slowly forward.

The horse stepped gingerly, but the branches pressed down to pack tightly at once, and after another few tentative steps the horse moved out. Fargo saw the animal continue to move carefully, unhappy with the feel of the terrain under its feet, but it kept moving as Annabel coaxed it forward. Fargo watched, his eyes narrowed, and as the horse reached the other side of the trench, he beckoned the second wagon forward. Once again his gaze was riveted on the wheels of the heavier wagon as they began to roll across the tightly packed branches. The wagon dipped, sank, but only a little as the branches held together and the horses pulled forward despite their obvious uneasiness. He was still watching the packed branches dip yet cushion the wheels when, out of the corner of his eye, he glimpsed the red-orange arc. He whirled in time to see the flaming torch made of a piece of wood and kerosene-soaked rags whirling through the air. It had been flung from inside the nearby treeline at the other side of the trench, and when it landed on the branches, too many of them bone-dry, the sheet of flame exploded skyward instantly.

Fargo saw Seth Crowler, halfway across the trench, freeze and rein back as he stared at the flames that began to consume the branches with instant fury.

"Go on, dammit, go on," Fargo shouted at the man. "Keep going." With the admonition still in the air the Trailsman sprang onto the branches and raced to where the fire had already established itself at the edge of the tightly packed wood. He began to pull up the nearest branches and throw them away, attacking the wood with feverish haste. "Give me a hand," he yelled over his shoulder.

Crowler's horses, suddenly panicked by the flames, drove forward and reached the other side of the trench and the firm land there. Vivian appeared at Fargo's side and began to throw half-burning branches from the packed pile and then Thomas Turner and Humphrey Asgood reached him and began working as well. Others came up and Fargo finally called a halt when all the burning material had been thrown aside to burn out by itself in the trench.

He drew a deep breath and stared at the remaining bed of branches still bridging the trench. It was but half as wide as it had been and the wagon wheels would just barely fit.

From the other side, Annabel called to him as she saw him studying the trench. "Shall we start filling it up again?" she asked.

"No, it'll take another day to get everything packed in again," Fargo called back. "Besides, I don't want to wait here another night and give him a chance to really burn it all while we're asleep. We're going on." He turned and waved to Terrall, who looked on from the side. "Cross over and see if you can flush him out of those trees,' he ordered, and stood back while Terrall led his men across the branches.

The next wagon in line held two families with three children, and Fargo ordered everyone out but the driver, a strong-armed man named Bettledorf. "Straight and steady," Fargo called, and watched the two wheels on his side edge the end of the branches. Again, the horses were uneasy at the footing, but Bettledorf had a good hand on the reins and a good way with his voice. The team moved forward with careful slowness and Fargo's lips pulled back in satisfaction as the bed of branches held together and the wagon reached the other side.

He waved the others on and they each crossed with slow caution. The bed of branches held up and it was almost dusk when all the wagons had reached the other side.

Terrall returned with his men and met Fargo's questioning glance. "No sign of anybody," the man said. "He must've hightailed it."

"Hell he did," Fargo grunted. "Take your positions. We're going on." There was still traveling time left in the day and he climbed onto the Ovaro.

Annabel called to him as he came abreast of her

wagon and he slowed. "You could be wrong. They would've found him if he were hiding nearby. Maybe he decided to run," she said.

"Terrall didn't look hard," Fargo snapped. He saw annoyance in Annabel's expression.

"You certainly cling to your suspicions, don't you?" she tossed at him.

He answered by spurring the Ovaro forward into a trot and riding on. As he rode, he slowed, broke off the end of new, young branches to mark the way. He rode with his gaze sweeping the terrain, but the light was almost gone and he soon found a place where the trees thinned out and the wagons could come to a halt among them. He waited and guided them into the forest. Supper was simple, beans heated quickly and some beef strips, everyone plainly weary from the day's ordeal.

Vivian passed nearby with a pail of water and he stepped out from behind one of the wagons.

"You were real good today," he said. "You were the first to jump in."

"Seemed like the thing to do," she said, and followed with a smile that held both warmth and slyness in it. "Besides, I didn't want to see anything happen to you, trying to do it all alone."

"Thanks," Fargo smiled.

She hurried on, her dark eyes still dancing with their own deep fires. Fargo took his bedroll to the side, nested down under the branches of an alder, and quickly drew sleep around himself.

He woke early, dressed, and took a mug of coffee from Harriet Crowler as the others only began to emerge from their wagons. He was on the Ovaro as Annabel appeared and he paused beside her.

"I'll mark the trail," he said. "Get moving." He hurried off into the low hills and explored the mountain forest, slowing his pace and marking a twisted trail through terrain that would allow the wagons. It was noon when he halted at a mountain stream and let the pinto drink and cool his ankles while the wagons finally rolled up.

He allowed nearly an hour's rest before moving on, and the day had moved into midafternoon when he caught the movement along the trail behind. He halted and backed the pinto into the thick woods. His hand was on the Colt at his hip when Vivian Starr came into sight on a brown horse. He moved from the trees and she halted beside him.

"Thought I'd ride some with you," she said, and he took in the deep-breasted curve of her that filled the gray shirt she wore, and the eyes that seemed unable not to smolder.

"Just for company's sake?" He smiled and moved the Ovaro forward.

"No," she admitted with a half-sheepish smile. "I wondered if you'd thought about our talk, about the things I asked you."

"Some," he said. "Let's see how we both feel when the time comes for me to leave."

"I know how I'll feel."

"We'll see," Fargo said calmly.

"And I'm still afraid, Fargo," Vivian said almost angrily. "I wake up at least once a night in a cold sweat."

He frowned at her words but made no reply as his eyes went out to the thick, green dark of the mountains while he moved on. They were nearing the top edge of the low hills and the ruggedness of the mountain range glowered down at them. He rode on, perhaps another hour or more, and saw the day beginning to fade. Then he halted, leaned down out of the saddle, and scooped up a wrist gauntlet that lay on the ground. He examined the workmanship on the thin leather, the design cut in by a procupine quill. "Northern Shoshoni," he murmured, his eyes sweeping the mountain forests. But only a soft wind disturbed the foliage and he rode on, Vivian staying close.

The daylight had dwindled down to near dusk when he found a place where a small mountain pond made a circle of coolness a dozen yards away through the trees. "You stay here," he said to Vivian, and sent the Ovaro up a steep incline until he reached a place that let him stand out in the open as he looked down at the terrain below.

He waited and finally the wagons appeared through a break in the trees, following the trail he had marked out for them. He lifted an arm and waved and saw Annabel glimpse him and wave back. He waited and made certain they turned along the right passage before he rode back down to Vivian. "They'll be another half-hour reaching us," he said. "I'm going to wash off some trail sweat." He took a towel from his saddlebag, walked through the trees to the little pond, and undressed, putting the Colt right at the edge of the water. He stretched his magnificently muscled form and started to go into the pond when his ears caught the sound of brush being parted. He continued into the water and kept the smile inside himself.

The pond—spring-fed, he discovered—was delightfully cool. He floated, enjoying himself in the water as he felt eyes on him. When he finally emerged and began to dry himself, he heard the bushes rustle again, more hastily this time. Finally dried and dressed, he returned to the campsite, where Vivian leaned against a tree. Her smoldering eyes held on him as he hung the towel on a tree to dry.

"Why didn't you join me instead of just watching?" he asked, looking at her only when he finished the question. Surprise flashed across her broad face.

It took her a moment to recover and a half-smile crept across her lips. "I knew the others could arrive at any minute," she answered. "And I knew what they'd find me doing."

"That's honest enough," Fargo admitted. Anything more was cut off as he saw her pull back words when the green Baker's wagon appeared and rolled past to the end of the site Fargo had chosen. The other wagons followed and Vivian took her horse and tied it to the back of her wagon as Herb Starr pulled to a stop.

Supper was quickly prepared and again Fargo saw that Terrall and his men stayed to themselves during the meal, but he found Annabel beside him when he finished his meal.

"Vivian Starr seems to be getting very friendly with you," she commented.

"Nothing wrong in being friendly," Fargo answered evenly.

"No, if that's where it stays," Annabel said with a sudden sharpness in her voice.

"Why, Annabel, you've a suspicious turn of mind," Fargo said.

"I heard quite enough about the rest of your reputation," she said with an edge of disapproval. "I don't think Herb Starr likes the idea of his wife going off to ride with you. But I don't suppose what a husband thinks bothers you any."

"It might, if he were a proper husband," Fargo said.

"Meaning what?" Annabel questioned with one eyebrow lifting.

"I'm told that's no marriage. She's a prisoner and a servant, not a wife," Fargo said.

Annabel took in his words for a moment, but her face stayed tight. "No matter. I want you to keep your attentions on other things."

"You speaking up for yourself?" Fargo grinned and drew an instant glare.

"I'm speaking about doing what you were hired to do . . . and nothing else," she snapped.

"I'll try to remember that," Fargo said.

Annabel whirled away. Fargo took his bedroll into the trees behind the wagons, undressed in the warm night, and peered out at the outline of the mountains edged in moonlight. An eerie stillness held the air, as though the usual prowlers of the night were afraid to stir. The frown on his brow stayed as he went to sleep.

When morning came with a burning sun, he rose and dressed and waited only for the others to wake up enough to see him ride into the hills. He marked a trail for the wagons as he rode, and when noon came, he halted at a stream and let the others catch up.

Vivian came to fill her canteen beside him and tossed him a sidelong smile.

"Seems your husband was upset when you went off to ride with me yesterday," Fargo said.

"Doesn't bother me any," Vivian said. "He tell you that?"

"No. Annabel did," Fargo answered.

Vivian's smile took on a private wisdom. "Maybe she's the one that was upset," Vivian murmured.

"Come, now, Annabel's only concern is her nature studies," Fargo said.

"Don't bet on it," Vivian said. "She's all female under that dedication."

Fargo frowned at Vivian's back as the woman walked back to her wagon. He turned, swung onto the Ovaro again, and waved the wagons forward. He rode on and had gone perhaps another two hours when he spotted the line of near-naked horsemen suddenly appear on the high ground. He halted and peered up at the riders and had just counted twenty when Annabel and the others rolled up.

"Northern Shoshoni," Fargo said as Annabel stared up at the bronzed figures on their short-legged ponies. He smiled at the alarm in her hazel eyes. "They're just looking. Window-shopping, you might say," he murmured.

"How do you know?" Annabel asked apprehensively.

"They'll want more company before they mount an attack."

"What do we do?" she asked.

"We keep on and keep alert," Fargo answered.

He saw Terrall and his men nervously peering up at the Indians. The Trailsman waved the wagons forward, and the line of Shoshoni moved in and out of sight until they finally faded away. Fargo spurred the Ovaro forward and rode on ahead of the others. He halted when he came to a wide passage. He peered at the ground and the low brush that grew at the sides of the passage and saw something else: the deep marks of wagon wheels leading up into the wide trail.

Annabel rolled up as he stared at the earth and the wide passage. He saw her instant frown as he motioned away from the trail and into the thick forest land.

"That way looks considerably easier," Annabel

said, and nodded at the wide passage. "And look at those wagon tracks. The Hostler wagons, probably."

"Probably," Fargo agreed calmly. "We go that way," he said. She opened her mouth to protest when his eyes fastened on her. "You want to take over breaking trail?" he slid at her. Her lips tightened and she swallowed the words, snapped the reins, and followed him as he led the way under low branches that scraped the canvas tops of the wagons.

He steered his way through a very narrow trail that twisted and turned every five minutes and hugged the base of a long, sloping hill. It became a tortuous passage through the remainder of the day. Dusk began to slide down the mountain when Fargo pulled to a halt at a flat half-circle of land and waited for the others to roll up.

As Annabel swung down from her baker's wagon, he motioned to her and she followed as he walked another fifty yards or so forward. He halted and pointed to the line of broken tree limbs and skidding, rutted wagon-wheel marks that went down a steep hillside. "The Hostler wagons," he said. "They had to come down the hard way."

"How'd you know?" Annabel asked, her voice small.

"That wide passage was a rainwash. It had to end abruptly somewhere above in a wall of rock and earth," Fargo said. He peered at the wagon-wheel marks again. "I'd guess they lost a day, maybe two, repairing wheel and axle damage." He looked at Annabel, the waiting in his lake-blue yes.

"I guess I was smart to hire you, wasn't I?" she said with a tart smile, and started to leave. He watched her flounce away with more swing to her rear than he'd seen before. He grinned as he turned and slowly followed her back to the wagons.

Some of the women had supper on already and he took the tin plate of beans and beef strips handed him and sat down to the side. Terrall and his men were at the far end of the camp, still keeping to themselves, he noted. When he finished the meal, he turned his plate in and walked to the Ovaro and took his bedroll down. He started to walk away with it when Vivian appeared in the long gray dress.

"Where will you be?" she asked softly.

"Straight up the slope behind you," he told her. "Why?"

"I'm feeling restless," she murmured.

He watched her move away quickly and waited till she reached her wagon before he went on up the slope. He climbed the tree-covered hill and finally halted at the broad base of an alder. There he set down his bedroll, undressed to his underwear, and stretched out. They'd be full into the mountains come tomorrow, he realized, and he was growing more concerned about Dick Terrall. The man would make his move soon. He had no reason to risk going much deeper into the mountains, especially after seeing the Shoshoni. But Terrall would want him out of the way first, Fargo was certain, and his lips grew tight as thoughts revolved inside him.

They broke off as he heard the sound of the figure carefully moving up the hill. He sat up and saw the moonlight catch the cheekbones of the broad face. He rose and let her find him.

Vivian Starr hurried forward and he was seated on the bedroll when she reached him. She came down onto her knees beside him and he took in the smoldering attractiveness of her, full, deep breasts pressed against the gray dress to bulge out over the neckline.

"Guess you're still restless," he remarked.

"More than that, Fargo. Between being scared inside every night and seeing those Shoshoni today, I came to get one thing out of this trip before it's too late," Vivian said with anger in her voice. "I don't expect you have to ask what that is."

"Guess not," Fargo said softly, and watched her open the top buttons of the dress. Her breasts spilled out at once, deeper and fuller than they seemed under the fabric, just edging flabbiness yet still strong, very white with large deep pink areolae and firm, already erect nipples of red-brown. She slid the remainder of the dress down, revealing a waist with a slight bulge of extra flesh, a rounded belly, and a deep tangle of blackness at the juncture of full yet curving thighs. Vivian Starr had a body that still held itself together with the same smoldering quality that was echoed in her eyes, and she brought the warmth of herself against him as he lay back. Her breasts, very soft, flattened against his chest, and her mouth opened on his with almost desperate hunger.

Her tongue darted out, probed, pulled back, and came forward again, a hot, stabbing messenger of wanting. He heard her soft groan of pleasure as he responded, rolled with her, and his hand curled around one large, deep breast. He pressed and caressed, running his thumb gently back and forth across the firm red-brown tip. Vivian groaned, a deep cry of satisfaction that seemed to rise from the pit of her stomach. He took his lips from hers and sank them onto one deep, pillowy mound. He drew as much of it as he could into his mouth and felt the firm nipple press against the roof of his mouth. He pulled, sucked, caressed with his tongue, and felt Vivian's full-fleshed body twist in delight. "Oh,

Jeeez, yes, yes . . . so long, oh, so long," she moaned. "Go on, go on . . . oh, God, yes."

He used his hands to caress the other breasts, then moved down across her waist to press firmly into the rounded belly. Vivian's hips continued to twist and writhe and she groaned out the deep, visceral sighs of contentment and pleasure. His hand moved down, through the black, tangled, soft-wire nap, and pressed the rounded pubic mound. He felt Vivian's hips lift against his touch. "Aaaaaagh," she groaned. He felt her hand come down on top of his, her fingers clutch at him pulling his hand down to the wet warmth of her.

"Don't make me wait, Fargo, please," Vivian gasped. "Take me . . . oh, God, yes, yes . . ." He probed, his fingers sliding across the wet, viscous path to enter and rub gently along the luscious, soft walls. Vivian moaned and her legs fell open, her thighs quivering.

The dark, deep groans rose and fell with their own rhythm as he touched, pressed, explored, and when he lifted his body to lie atop her, she cried out with renewed eagerness. "Yes, oh, damn, damn, yes . . . now, now," Vivian cried with a fervent urgency in her voice. Her desperate wanting was its own kind of excitement and he let himself slide into her, his own self pulsating with warmth.

Vivian's voice rose into an instant half-scream. "Oh, my God, my God, aaaaaaaagh . . . aaaah, ah, ah, aaaaah," she gasped out, and there was no reserve in her half-sobbed pleasure. He felt her ample hips lift and her body began to thrust upward at once—quick, hurried pumpings as though time would race away, each motion accompanied by a short groaned gasp. Vivian's hands dug into his back and pulled him down to her so his face fell into the deep valley between her breasts.

He let himself revel in their pillowy softness as his mouth groped across the twin mounds for the soft-firm tips, and Vivian half-screamed again. He felt her torso begin to twist and her hands dig harder into his back. Her upward pumping became a quaking crescendo and her voice called out of some deep cavern of ecstasy. "Now, Fargo . . . now. It's now. Now . . . ah, aaaaah . . . oh, Jesus." He felt her full, soft thighs clasp around his waist, a pillowed vice as the surging climax coursed through her. She pressed his face down onto her breasts as if she could somehow make flesh meld with flesh. Her groans were fashioned of deep, dark ecstasy, murmurings out of a primeval need too long unsatisfied, and she clung to him, her entire body quaking, long after the moment had exploded and vanished. Finally, with a despairing sigh, she collapsed under him but continued to hold his face against her breasts.

"God, that was great," Vivian breathed, and Fargo pulled up to peer into her dark, smoldering eyes. "It's been too long. I won't wait so long again, ever."

"Guess not," Fargo said.

"You've got to take me with you when you go back, Fargo," the woman said, pressing her body against his. "I'll make it worth your while, I promise."

"I imagine you will," he said. "But there's plenty of time for deciding about that."

Vivian's broad face turned with a frown and she peered hard at him. "You don't think we're going to make it. Leastwise not all of us. Maybe you don't have dreams or premonitions, but that's what you feel, isn't it?"

"Sometimes," he said. "I keep hoping I'm wrong. Or that I can do something about it. I'll ride with that till I know different."

The seriousness of her broad face gave way to a sudden smile and her arms slide around his neck. "Then I'll just have to find another time and another place real soon," Vivian said, lifting her large, deep breasts and pressing them into his face. Suddenly, she spun from him with surprising lightness. She stood up, a large woman, everything about her large and fulsome and fashioned of earthy attractiveness.

He enjoyed watching her pull the dress on, her every movement one of mature sensuousness, and he rose when she finished for another embrace.

"Till next time," she murmured, and he watched her go down the hill until she disappeared into the darkness.

He folded himself onto the bedroll when a howl drifted through the night from the distant mountain slopes. Unmistakably a wolf's howl, there was something very different about it, a quality he could not quickly define yet had never heard before. It came but once, lingered distantly in the air, and then the night fell silent again.

Fargo lay back, closed his eyes, and slept till the morning brought the warm yellow sun.

= 5 =

Fargo strolled down the slope and paused to take in the beauty of a long circle of fringed gentian that formed a blue-violet necklace around the hill. When he reached the wagons, he made for the Ovaro to one side and tied his things onto the saddle. He saw Humphrey Asgood's rounded figure beside David Corry and Avery Hodges as the three men sipped coffee. He had started toward where Harriet Crowler tended the coffeepot when he saw Annabel striding toward him, her apple-cheeked face set in fury.

"Over here," she hissed at him, and led the way to the side where her baker's wagon rested. "How could you?" She whirled at him from behind the wagon.

"How could I what?" Fargo frowned.

"Don't play games with me, Fargo. You know what I'm talking about," Annabel accused.

He kept his face expressionless as he met her angry glare. "Spell it out, honey," he said.

"Sleeping with Vivian Starr, that's what," Annabel flung at him, her eyes hazel flame.

"Now where'd you get that from?"

"Herb Starr. It seems he was awake when she came strolling back in the wee hours of the morning," Annabel returned, ice on each word.

"Maybe he's jumping to conclusions," Fargo said.

"*Hah!* None that I wouldn't jump to."

Fargo shrugged. "Guess you've both got the same problem, suspicious minds."

"He told me that if I didn't send you packing he'd have to kill you," Annabel said.

"What'd you answer?" Fargo asked mildly.

"I told him I couldn't send you packing. I needed you, I said. And he, too," Annabel answered. "I don't think he liked that answer."

Fargo recalled how Vivian had told him her husband was a back-shooter, but he wanted to calm down Annabel's fears first. "He'll simmer down. He enjoys talking big, I hear," he said soothingly.

"Damn you, Fargo. Why didn't you listen to me? Ever hear of refusing? Saying no?" Annabel snapped.

"Turning down someone in need is a sin. The Good Book says that." He smiled and saw Annabel's hand come up to strike at him. He caught her wrist as her eyes blazed fury at him. "Temper, temper," he murmured. He took his hand from her wrist as he felt her arm relax and she took a step back.

"Dammit, Fargo, you find a way to settle this without more trouble," she demanded. She whirled and strode away and Fargo let the casual half-smile drop from his face. There'd be no easy way to settle this, he knew, not with the likes of Herb Starr. The man was too steeped in his own twisted ways. Vivian's description of him made it plain that he enjoyed the pleasures of mastery and cowardly revenge. Fargo uttered a silent oath as he saddled the Ovaro and led the horse past the wagons. He saw Vivian emerge from hers and meet his eyes with an almost smug smile.

"He give you a hard time last night?" Fargo asked.

"He knows better than that," Vivian said.

"I hear he's mighty unhappy," Fargo said.

"That doesn't bother me any, but you take special care," the woman said, concern sudden in her voice. Fargo nodded as he climbed onto the Ovaro and Vivian returned to her wagon. He saw Herb Starr emerge to take the reins of the team, the man studiously avoiding him.

Fargo turned his horse and began to ride north. Perhaps it was just as well, he told himself. He'd already made a decision about Terrall and Barrat Dowling. He might just as well include Herb Starr. He turned as he rode and saw Terrall and his men take their positions alongside the wagons.

He'd decided he couldn't afford to wait any longer for Terrall to make his move. He'd trigger the man into action, and perhaps Dowling, too. Now there was one more to add. Fargo's lips pursed as he rode. The hardest part would be to fake reality, he pondered. No crude makeshift arrangements would do for this. His mouth tightened as he realized that perhaps there was no other way but that. His lips stayed tight as he turned plans in his mind while he moved along the passage and his eyes swept the land on all sides. He grew increasingly unhappy as he could come up with nothing to satisfy himself, and he finally broke off thoughts and halted until Annabel caught up with him.

The wheel marks of the Hostler wagons remained clear on up the passage through the forest, none of the inclines too steep, he could see, and he brought the pinto alongside her. "Follow the wagon tracks. I'll meet up with you later," he told her, avoiding questions by quickly sending the Ovaro into a trot.

He rode north, along the passage, until he was comfortably out of sight, then he swerved into the thick forest and doubled back the way he had come. He passed where they had camped for the night and continued on until he finally turned again and made his way back to the passage.

The Trailsman slowed, carefully edged his way out onto the trail, and his eyes swept the ground until he picked up the hoofprints of a single horse moving carefully behind the last of the wagon tracks. He saw the hoofprints go on for a few dozen yards and then turn into the heavy forest land. Barrat Dowling was being both persistent and clever. He'd follow and then move into the thick forest terrain until it was time to return to the passage again. Moving back and forth, following, observing, moving from the low ground to the high, he was keeping the wagons under observance at all times and himself out of sight. Fargo grunted. He'd underestimated Dowling. The Trailsman moved forward in the trees and his eyes peered through the foliage to the high ground on the other side of the passage until he finally spotted the lone horseman move into an open place for a brief moment and then vanish again.

Satisfied he'd made no mistake, Fargo sent the Ovaro into a trot, and a grim smile touched his lips. He'd let Dowling's determined observance work for him, he promised himself as he rode on. He stayed in the heavy forest terrain as he caught up to and passed the wagons. He rode on and swung back to the passage a few hundred yards on. The wheel marks of the Hostler wagons were still clear along the passage and he reined up and swung to the ground to run his fingers along the tops of the rutted edges. "Four days old, maybe five," he muttered aloud, and climbed back onto the pinto. He rode on, spied a steep path to the right just wide enough for a single horse, and sent the Ovaro upward until he reached a flat place that let him look over the terrain.

Ahead and below, he saw the line of Shoshoni warriors riding easily along a ridge. He counted twenty, again. They hadn't added more yet, he saw with gratefulness. He let his eyes move north and halt at an open, flat area surrounded by only the blackened stumps of fire-ravaged trees. But new saplings had already begun to sprout and it made a good spot for the wagons to camp for the night. It was also a place Barrat Dowling could easily observe from the thickness of the nearby trees. Fargo took the horse back down the incline and met the wagons as they rolled up.

"This way," he said, and swung alongside Annabel's wagon as he led the way in a slow circle. Little beads of perspiration covered her face, he saw, and her apple cheeks glistened, yet she somehow managed to look attractive. Her shirt, damp with perspiration, lay against the curve of her breasts to outline each almost as if she'd nothing on. He enjoyed the beauty of her. She saw the smile in his eyes as he watched her breasts sway with the motion of the wagon, and she fastened him with a cool glance.

"You ought to be thinking about apologizing to Herb Starr," she tossed at him.

"Waste of time," he told her.

"So you're going to do nothing?"

"Didn't say that," Fargo answered, and spurred the pinto forward. He waved Annabel's wagon under a canopy of low branches that opened onto a reasonable resemblance of a road.

Something lay on the ground a dozen yards ahead and he rode on. He had just dismounted and stared down at a collection of shovels and pickaxes, all scattered on the ground along with a knapsack and a bridle, as Annabel came up. Frowning, Fargo let his eyes sweep the ground nearby, and he saw part of a horse's leg half-hidden in the brush.

"Had to belong to a prospector," Fargo said. "Along with what's left of his horse."

"My God," Annabel whispered, and David Corry and Avery Hodges walked up, frowns on their faces.

"What happened to him?" Corry asked.

"God knows." Fargo shrugged as he continued to stare at the objects littering the ground.

"An Indian attack? The Shoshoni got him?" Hodges suggested.

"No," Fargo said. "They'd have gone through his pack, taken the tools, too."

"There's no trace of him here. Animals drag him off?"

"Could have. That's what happened to most of his horse," Fargo said. He pointed to the marks in the dirt, and the frown still on his brow, he carefully stepped across the ground. The frown dug deeper into his brow as he picked out the footprints, heels deep into the soil. "He backed up here," Fargo said, following the prints. "He was backing away from something." Fargo paused and leaned forward as he saw the prints change in the soil. "He turned here, started running." Fargo quickened his pace as he followed the footprints to the trunk of a low-branched bur oak. He halted at the base of the tree, looked up into the branches, and heard the oath fall from his lips. "Goddman," he breathed as he stared up at the body wedged in the branches of the tree.

"Oh, God," Annabel breathed directly behind him, and he saw she'd followed on his heels. She gazed up into the tree and Corry and Hodges came up to stare in shock.

"Help me get him down," Fargo said, and swung himself into the tree on the nearest thick branch, pulled up on the next, and was beside the lifeless, stiff figure. He dislodged the body from where it was wedged in the crook of a branch, lowered it with one hand to Hodges and Corry, and the two men lifted it to the ground. Fargo leapt lithely from the tree and landed beside Annabel. Some of the others had come up to stare at the man, and Fargo looked down at a white-bearded, white-haired figure of medium build. But it was the man's eyes that held him. In death, they still stared with a terrible terror.

"Something put the fear of God into him," Fargo said.

"He's not marked in any way. No arrows in him," David Corry said. "No Indian attack, as you said."

"Then, what?" Annabel questioned.

"I can piece some of it together," Fargo said. "He ran from something, took to the tree for safety. His heart gave out while he was in the tree, maybe from fear, maybe from exertion, or maybe it was just ready to give out. In any case, he stayed wedged there." Fargo paused, frowned down at the stiff figure whose eyes stared with terror in death, still mirroring the last emotion he had felt in life. Fargo glanced at Annabel. "The little girl I found, out of the Frawley wagon, her eyes held the same terror," he said.

Annabel's frown gathered slowly and she stared back. "What are you saying?"

"I'm not saying, but I'm wondering real hard," Fargo answered. "I just wish I knew what I should be wondering about."

"We should bury the poor man," he heard Vivian say, and nodded. He kept his face expressionless while thoughts raced inside him. Perhaps fate had handed him a grim solution to the problem he had wrestled with through the day.

"We've no time for digging a proper place," he said. "Cut down a dozen branches." He reached down and began to pull the old prospector into the trees at the side of the path, and when the branches were cut, he fashioned a funeral bower, Indian-fashion, over the body. When he was finished, pushing down the sourness inside him, he led the wagons forward to the flat land that had once been fire-swept. A bed of new, soft grama grass had carpeted the surface and formed a good place to camp.

Fargo let the wagons roll to a halt, waited till Dick Terrall and his men were nearby, and almost smiled as Annabel's question came with perfect, if unplanned, timing.

"Aren't we stopping a little early? There's at least an hour of daylight left," she asked.

"Two reasons: this is a good place to make camp, and I'm riding up into the center of that hill," Fargo said, and pointed to the mountainside directly ahead. "I'm going to stay the night there, make myself a little fire later, and bed down. I want to be in the high land, come dawn. I want to see if I can find where the Shoshoni are coming from."

Annabel nodded and Fargo caught the quick exchange of glances between Terrall and his men. He saw Herb Starr beside his wagon, the man's dour, stern face impassive, and Fargo turned the pinto north and slowly rode from the camp. Starr had been close enough to hear everything, and Terrall had barely suppressed his anticipation. Fargo was also certain that Barrat Dowling would see him ride from the campsite alone. Dowling would follow to be certain where he went while the light permitted.

Fargo let the pinto slowly climb up through the

heavy brush and foliage of the mountainside. He held a steady pace and a straight line until the darkness came to cloak him and the mountainside. If Barrat Dowling had followed, he'd settle down to wait, Fargo was certain. If his quarry stayed shrouded in the night, he'd make his way back to where the wagons were camped. If not, he'd try to seize his chance. Terrall would send his killers along later, Fargo mused, and Herb Starr was an extra question mark.

Fargo turned the pinto into the trees to his right as the moon rose to filter weakly into the forest. He sent the horse back down the mountainside, riding slowly through the dense tree cover, and he passed the spot where the wagons camped with a few hundred yards to spare. The grim distaste inside him grew stronger as he neared the spot where he'd left the body of the old prospector. It was a nasty, sour business, he admitted, but it had to be done, the grim offer too perfect to turn aside from, and when he reached the bower of branches, he dismounted and began to pull aside the leafy covering.

When he had cleared away enough, he pulled the old prospector's body free and deposited the stiff form across the saddle. "Maybe you never did a good deed in your life, old man," Fargo muttered. "Or maybe you did a lot of them. Either way, you're going to get to do one more now."

Fargo climbed onto the Ovaro and began the ride back north, staying clear of the fire-ravaged flat place where the wagons were camped and finally moving up the mountainside again. The grim passenger across the saddle almost slipped off twice, but Fargo caught the silent form each time and the distaste inside his stomach continued to churn. But conscience was one thing, reality another, he grimaced. He had to carry out his plan to the very best, and none of the makeshift ideas he had turned in his mind all day had held together.

The bullets that he felt certain would fly through the darkness had to land with the right sound. Those who fired them would be listening for the soft, thudding sound that would mean only one thing: their shots had landed in flesh and bone. And if they came closer, they'd see the stain of red. They had to feel satisfied they'd done their job, satisfied and relaxed enough so he could do his.

Fargo reined to a halt finally at a spot where the mountainside leveled off for a dozen yards. He dismounted and dragged the silent form from the saddle, put it on the ground in the darkness, and quickly pulled off his own jacket, shirt, and hat. He cursed silently as he struggled to put his clothes on the stiff body and had to crack one limb to finally finish. At last, he dragged the body against the base of a tree, leaned it back in a sitting slouch, and tied his hat down over the old prospector's face. Only then did he make the small fire that would be seen by those waiting and watching in the night darkness.

He took the Ovaro to one side, tethered the horse where it would be clearly visible, and then retreated into the thick brush, where he lay down on his stomach, the big Colt in one hand. If he had calculated correctly, Terrall would be watching from near the camp and move into action when he spied the flicker of light up on the mountainside. But Barrat Dowling would have followed more closely. He'd be the first to spot the fire, and the nearest. As for Herb Starr, he remained the question mark, and Fargo settled down to wait, every fiber of his being tuned to his task—sight, sound, scent, and touch. His eyes peered into the pale moonlight of the night, his ears picked up the faintest of sounds, his nose separated the forest odors, and his body, prone across the ground, responded to the movements of the night creatures that disturbed the soil.

Yet the sound, when it came, startled him with its total unexpectedness. The wolf's howl shattered the stillness, rose high in the air, and hung there until it finally subsided. It was still distant, yet considerably closer than it had been the night before. It had the same strange quality in it, unlike any wolf's howl he'd ever heard. It came again, hung high in the air, but there was menace, not mournfulness, in it, a call of command, an imperious warning out of the savage wild. The howl faded away and the stillness returned.

Fargo brought his attention back to the small scurrying nearby sounds and the moonlit mountainside. His attention was on two-legged marauders, not four-legged ones, and he lay silent and unmoving. The minutes seemed to drag on as though they were hours when suddenly he caught the sound of footsteps moving cautiously through the brush on the opposite side of the small fire.

Fargo's eyes narrowed as he strained to catch the sound again. One man, moving on careful steps, he discerned. He put the Colt down on the ground in front of him, reached to the holster around his calf, and drew out the double-edged throwing knife. He couldn't risk filling the mountainside with the sounds of a gunfight—not yet, anyway, he grunted. He rose up on one knee as the figure appeared through the brush, tall and lean, the smoldering firelight picking up the tight, lean face and long black hair of Barrat Dowling. It was a grim, sour kind of satisfaction Fargo felt surge inside him, and as he watched, Dowling stepped from the brush and Fargo saw he had a big Remington .44 rifle in his hands. The man raised the rifle to his shoulder, aimed, and fired. Fargo watched the bullets slam through his hat and into the face behind it.

"So much for you, Mr. Trailsman," Dowling muttered, bloodless triumph in his voice.

Fargo raised his arm, took aim, and let the razor-sharp double-edged blade hurtle through the air just as Dowling turned half around. The blade struck Dowling at the base of his neck and he stumbled, finished his turn, and his eyes stared at the figure of the big man that stepped from the trees. He managed to utter one word in a gasped, strangulated breath. "You . . ." he said, and sank to the ground on his knees. He reached a hand up, closed it around the handle of the throwing knife, but the last of his life force had already gone from him. He pitched forward to land facedown on the ground, his fingers still closed around the knife handle.

Moving quickly, Fargo ran to Dowling's body and dragged it into the blackness of the underbrush. He retrieved the throwing knife, wiped it clean on the soft moss under the brush, and hurried back to where he had waited in the thick foliage. His eyes held for a moment on the body against the base of the tree, the hat now only half-covering the face. It didn't matter, he saw. In his murderous efficiency, Barrat Dowling had done him a favor. His bullets had shattered the face beneath the hat into an unrecognizable morass of fragmented bone, torn flesh, and slow-seeping red.

Fargo settled down on one knee, once again tuning his every sense to the night. The wait was far shorter than the first had been, and he picked up the sound of the brush moving. Two figures this time, once again on the other side of the still-smoldering fire. They halted, still not in sight, and he followed the sound of them as they half-circled through the trees, moving carefully, to approach the still figure at the base of the tree from the front.

This time Fargo took the Colt back in hand as he saw the two figures halt at the edge of the bushes. Enough firelight still glimmered for him to recognize them as two of Terrall's men. One took another tentative step forward, his neck craning, and Fargo watched him stare at the still form by the tree.

"Jesus," the man murmured, and waved the other one forward. "Somebody's gone and done him in for us," he said. Fargo watched the two men come closer in quick, half-crouching steps. They halted some ten feet from the tree. "Christ, somebody blew his head off," the one said, awe in his voice.

"Let's get back and tell Dick," the other one said. "Won't make no difference to Dick that somebody else did it. All he wants is word that Fargo's out of the way."

The two men turned and ran back to where they had left their horses, and Fargo stayed in the brush. He listened to the sound of them riding away before he rose and holstered the Colt. He walked to the figure beside the tree and took back his shirt and jacket but left the bullet-torn and bloodstained hat. He made a mental note to charge Annabel for a new hat, and turned and made his way into the trees where he had hidden the Ovaro. He had intended to stay in hiding longer and see if Herb Starr showed up, but that was out of the question now. It was plain that Terrall had decided to move against Annabel as soon as his two killers reported back to him. Fargo pulled on his clothes as he reached the horse, climbed into the saddle, and began to make his way down the mountainside.

He didn't hurry. He wanted to give Terrall time to

make his move so Annabel would have the proof in front of her. He rode with measured steps, peering through the trees as he did. He was halfway down the mountainside when he spotted the silhouetted form of the lone horse and rider moving up through the trees. Herb Starr would have to wait for another time and place, Fargo remarked silently, and turned the Ovaro sharply to the right to circle past the man. He had only gone a dozen feet when the horse stepped on a length of dry branch. It cracked with the sharpness of a rifle shot in the stillness, and Fargo swore silently. There was no time for a confrontation with Herb Starr now, but the sound had snapped the man's attention to him. He glanced back just in time to see the man's hand come up. Fargo flung himself sideways from the saddle as Herb Starr's shot slammed into a nearby tree. He hit the ground, rolled, and came up on one knee, the Colt in his hand.

It hadn't been a shot in the back but it had been a close try—a shot fired without certainty who the target was. Fargo stayed crouched silently as Herb Starr moved his horse forward.

"You hold it right there, Fargo," Herb Starr called out, and Fargo remained silent. "If you ain't Fargo, you better call your name," Starr said menacingly.

"I've no time for you now, Starr," Fargo called. The man's answer was another quick shot. "Not now, dammit," Fargo called.

Another shot answered, this one close enough the make him duck. "You're not gonna get a next time, Fargo," Herb Starr shouted, and fired off two more shots that made Fargo throw himself prone and roll into the brush. Herb Starr darted forward, fired again, and pulled out a second gun for another shot.

Fargo swore at the man as he stayed low, aimed,

fired and Saw Herb Starr clutch at his hip as he cursed in pain. The man stumbled and Fargo's second shot sent the six-gun spinning out of his hand as he emitted another oath of pain.

"Goddamn," Herb Starr cursed, and dived to one side as he went down. But Fargo, standing now, paused, took aim, and fired again, and the man let out a cry of pain and doubled over to clutch at his foot. "Ow, Jesus, my foot . . . Jesus," he cursed, and held onto his left foot.

Fargo stepped forward, halted in front of the man, and saw the fear in Herb Starr's eyes as he twisted on the ground, clutching first at his foot, then his hip, and then pressing his one injured hand to his chest. "Any one of those could've been between your eyes," Fargo growled. The man swallowed hard and stared at the barrel of the big Colt. "I could've done Vivian a favor and blown you out of her life," the Trailsman added, raising the gun a fraction. "Maybe I will," he added.

"No. No, don't," Herb Starr said, and fear had replaced the dourness of his face. "I won't try anything again, I swear it," the man offered.

"Don't swear. It's not polite," Fargo muttered. "I'd do it, but Annabel needs one good carpenter. Stay off Vivian's back, too." He holstered the Colt, spun from the man, and hurried to the Ovaro. The promise had been born out of fear, he realized, and he gave it little real substance. Yet he knew Starr would think long and hard before trying to come at him again.

But Fargo had now taken away precious minutes, and he sent the Ovaro crashing down the mountainside with as much speed as he dared in the tree-filled darkness. Skirting tree trunks, cutting corners through every space he could find, he finally felt the land level off and he neared the open stand where the wagons were camped. The moonlight was stronger now, and he saw the wagons take shape in the night, Annabel's nearest, and the curse fell from his lips as he saw the rear door hanging open.

He reined up outside the door and leapt to the ground, his lips pulled back in a grimace. They'd dragged her out and taken her with them, but they'd taken no time to cover their tracks. Terrall felt secure, Fargo grunted as he swung back onto the Ovaro and followed the broad trail up a side passage that rose at the edge of the burned-out land. He heard the short scream, Annabel's voice, cut off by a sharp slap, and he skidded the horse to a halt and landed on the ground on the balls of his feet. He caught the flicker of firelight a few hundred yards on and made for it in a crouching run.

The figures came into view, gathered around a low fire, and he saw Dick Terrall in front of Annabel. Two men held her on her knees on the ground, arms pulled behind her back, her breasts pressed tight against the thin fabric of the nightgown she wore.

"The money, goddammit," Terrall roared. "Where is it?"

"Go to hell," Annabel flung back.

"She wants to play hard," Terrall snarled. "Get a stick out of the fire."

One of the others stepped to the small fire and the two holding Annabel pushed her onto her back on the ground. She tried to kick out and only succeeded in revealing long, beautifully curved legs.

"Let's have us some fun with her first, Dick," one of the men said.

"No, we get the money first. Then you can have your way with her," Terrall said.

Fargo's eyes swept the men with a long hard

glance. Terrall and the two holding Annabel were nearest. Four more had formed a half-circle around them, and he saw three more standing off to one side.

"Give me the damn stick," Terrall called out impatiently.

"Wait a minute, Dick" Fargo heard one of the others call out, and he saw it was one of the three who watched from the side, a thin-framed man in a light-tan stetson. "We didn't sign up for any torturing. You said all we had to do was grab the money and run," the man said. "Jake, Harry, and me, we don't like this."

Fargo watched Terrall glare at the three men. "Then get the hell out of here," Terrall boomed. "You been paid. Hit the saddle. It'll leave more for the rest of us to split."

The three exchanged uncomfortable glances, yet Fargo saw a doggedness come into their faces. "We're no torturers, that's all," the tan-hatted one said. "We'd like our split, but we draw the line on this kind of stuff." The man paused, groped for words. "Why don't we just give her some more time to come around?"

"We don't have time, and her kind won't come around," Terrall snapped. "Now shut up or move out." The other man handed him the stick and Terrall brought the still-glowing end down to Annabel and held it not more than six inches from her breasts. "Now, I'm going to give you one more chance or you're going to really know about hot tits," he said.

Fargo saw terror finally come into Annabel's apple-cheeked face. She seemed transfixed as she stared at the glowing end of the piece of wood, unable to speak, her eyes growing wider in stark terror.

"All right, you've had it, sister," Terrall snarled,

and started to push the red-hot, glowing stick at her right breast.

"No," Annabel screamed, her voice tearing from her. "My wagon. Under the rear floorboards."

Terrall laughed and tossed the glowing stick aside. "Three of you come with me. The rest of you take your fun with her," he said, and started to turn away. Fargo's eyes swept the scene again. There were ten in all and he knew he couldn't take out all of them with one burst of gunfire. But he'd take out the top, he decided. That could be enough. If not, he'd battle it out with the others. He raised the Colt, took aim at Dick Terrall as the man climbed into the saddle. He waited till Terrall was straight on the horse before firing, a single shot that blew Terrall out of the saddle. But Fargo was whirling before Terrall hit the ground, the Colt barking twice at the two men who had hold of Annabel. Both let go of her to clutch hands to their stomachs as they fell backward. Out of the corner of his eye, Fargo saw the three men that had protested to Terrall vault onto their horses and race away. But the other four had dropped to the ground, drawn their guns, and fired a fusillade of shots into the trees. Fargo flung himself prone and the shots whistled over his head. He fired off two more shots and one of the four pitched forward with a last groan. As he reloaded, Fargo saw the other three dive for cover in the trees on the other side of the fire. They threw another volley of shots at him, but they had separated, two of the shots coming from the right of the fire, one from the left.

Fargo crawled silently through the trees, circling the fire, his eyes moving to where Annabel lay on the ground. There'd been enough sense or fright in her to lay still, but now she began to push herself up. "Stay down," he shouted, and flung himself sideways as the fusillade of shots followed the sound of his voice and he heard the bullets smack into the ground. He came up against the base of a tree, held his fire, and stayed motionless.

The trio across from him had neither the emotional nor mental discipline to use waiting as a weapon. It wouldn't be long before they made a move, Fargo was certain, and he waited with the Colt ready to fire. It wasn't more than a few minutes when the volley of shots exploded all around him. He dropped and flattened himself beside the tree and glimpsed the lone figure race from the brush toward where Annabel lay. They were laying a covering fire to let him seize her as a hostage, Fargo realized, but their fusillades were all too high.

He stayed flattened on the ground and took aim as the racing figure reached Annabel. The man was just reaching for her when Fargo fired, a single shot, and the man toppled forward, fell across the girl as she gave a half-scream. He lay still and the covering fire broke off and the mountainside grew silent.

Fargo saw Annabel sit up, uncertain whether to stay or try to run. The two men in the bush were silent for a few moments more, but Fargo knew it would not be for more than those few moments. He began to run through the trees in a crouch, moving with the swift silence of a mountain lion on the attack. Suddenly the two figures exploded in a flurry of snapping twigs and rustling bushes as they began to flee. Stepping only on the balls of his feet, Fargo circled the dying fire and was opposite the horses when the two men reached them. He stepped out of the brush, his voice almost soft. "Drop your guns. It's over," he said.

The two figures halted, focused on him, and the first one went into a crouch. "Like hell," the man muttered, and brought his gun up. Fargo's shot tore his midsection into a shower of red-stained tissue and intestines. The other man got off a shot that was too hasty. It missed Fargo's figure by six inches, and it was the last shot he ever fired as the big Colt barked. The man half-turned as he staggered backward, uttered a broken groan, and crumpled to the ground.

Fargo turned and walked toward Annabel, who had pushed herself to her feet. She ran toward him and fell against him before he was halfway to her, and he felt the trembling of her as well as the soft warmth of her breasts. Her hands pressed tight against his chest until she finally shook away the trembling and stepped back.

"Thank you," she murmured, her hazel eyes filled with relief and something else—chagrin, perhaps, he decided.

"That's not the way to say it." He smiled and drew a frown. "This is the way," he added, and brought his lips down over hers. She didn't pull away quickly and he felt her lips partly open, sweet softness, and then press closed as she pulled back.

"You can get that kind of thank-you from Vivian Starr," she said with a touch of primness. He shrugged and grinned at her. "But I am grateful," she said quickly. "You were right all along. I was lucky you changed your mind about spending the night on the mountain and came down at the exactly right moment."

"Luck had nothing to do with it, honey," he grunted. "Terrall sent two of his men up there to fill me with lead. Only I was waiting for them."

"That's why you told everyone where you'd be for the night," Annabel murmured. "You set a trap, with yourself as bait."

"Let's say I gave him an opportunity I knew he couldn't turn down," Fargo said. "And he wasn't the only one who took the bait. You won't be having any more trouble with Barrat Dowling." He smiled as he watched Annabel stare at him with a kind of awe. "I figured he might come running, too," Fargo said.

"You are remarkable," Annabel breathed.

"That mean you're ready to thank me proper?" He grinned.

She hesitated for a moment and then her chin turned upward. "No," she said righteously. "It'd be no, even if I wanted it to be yes."

"What in hell for?" Fargo frowned.

"It's called self-discipline, saying no, something you've never learned. It's paying heed to what's proper instead of what's satisfying."

"It's called being plain stupid," Fargo growled.

She tossed him a reproachful glare. "Get in the saddle. I'll take you back," he said with more gruffness than he'd intended.

But she quickly obeyed and he swung onto the horse behind her. He sent the pinto forward at a walk and the sides of her breasts pressed against his arms as he reached around her to hold the reins, very warm and very soft, and her rear moved against his crotch as they rode. She tried to hold herself away from him, but the movement of the horse made that impossible and he thought the trip down the hillside was pleasurably rewarding.

The camp was still hard asleep when they reached the wagons. He dismounted, reached up, and half-lifted her from the saddle, his hands folded around the curving warmth of her waist. When her feet touched the ground, he released his grip on her waist and her hazel eyes were suddenly soft.

"I am grateful, Fargo, and I'm sorry we don't have the same attitude on other things," she said.

"I'll give you another chance." He grinned.

She made a face and ignored the answer. "Will you stay here, close by?" she asked. "Three of Terrall's men did get away," she reminded him.

"They were backing off, anyway," he said. "I don't expect any trouble from those three. They had a streak of decency somewhere deep inside them."

"I'd still like you close by," she said with a half-shrug. "I'm frightened. I admit it."

"All right," he agreed.

She had turned and started into the long, close baker's wagon when the howl split the night, still distant and still holding the commanding, menacing core and still unlike the howl of any wolf he had ever heard. Annabel's eyes were wide, sudden fright in them.

"I've heard wolf howls before. This one is different," she said with a shudder.

"It is," Fargo agreed. "Not only the sound of it, either."

"What else?" she questioned.

"A wolf howls, usually there's an answer," Fargo said. "Or another wolf takes up the cry someplace. Not with this one."

"Maybe he's alone," Annabel offered.

"Not likely. Wolves are pack animals. That's one reason they call and answer one another. But this is no ordinary call. It's as though he's saying something and the others are all listening." Fargo frowned as the strange and menacing howl came again and finally drifted away into the darkness. He waited but that had been the end of it, and Annabel went into the wagon and pulled the rear door shut after her.

Fargo waited perhaps five minutes and then swung onto the tail step of the wagon, opened the door, and went inside.

She sat up instantly on a mattress neatly along one side of the wagon. "What are you doing?" she blurted.

"You said stay close by," he answered, and lowered himself onto the edge of the mattress and began to pull off boots.

"I didn't mean this close," Annabel snapped.

"I've always been bad on interpretation," Fargo said as he pulled off clothes and saw her eyes take in the muscled beauty of his chest and torso, his hips and stallionlike thighs. He undressed down to the bottoms of his underwear and stretched out on the mattress alongside her, but left at least a foot of space between them. "Make believe I'm not here," he said, and put his arms behind his head. He shot a glance at her and saw her eyes move down his body, linger on the bulge at his crotch, and return to his face. He lay back and closed his eyes. "Good night," he said, and the interior of the wagon grew almost still except for the harsh sound of her breathing. He heard her turn on her side, putting her back to him. He lay still, the tiny smile at the edge of his lips.

She lay for not more than a minute before turning back. He felt her eyes on him, but he remained motionless and suddenly he felt her hand touch his chest, a tentative touch, drawn away quickly and then put back again.

She let her hand stay on his chest, unmoving, and then slowly let it slide down across his body, touch against his ribs, slide back up along his pectorals.

"What's that mean?" he murmured, keeping his eyes closed.

"I don't know," Annabel said softly. "I just wanted to touch you."

He said nothing more. His eyes remained shut and he felt her hand move down across his chest again, a slow, warm touch, and he heard her stir, felt her move closer, and opened his eyes. She was against him, her breasts pushed hard against the smooth silk of the nightgown to create lovely, rounded cups. Her eyes went to his face and she rose up farther on one elbow and brought her face to his. He did nothing, let her move down, bring her lips against his, a sweet, gently eager kiss that she finally broke off. She looked down at him and he pushed onto his elbows and half-shrugged.

"Sorry," he said. "I can't." A tiny furrow moved across her brow. "I was told I had to learn to say no, to do what is proper, not what is satisfying."

"Damn you, Fargo," Annabel hissed, and her mouth came down over his again, harder this time, a sweet eagerness turned suddenly hungry, and he let his lips respond. She stayed, returned the touch of his tongue with her own darting smoothness, pulling back and coming forward, caressing his lips until she finally broke off and looked down at him from on her elbows. He reached up as she breathed hard, her breasts rising and falling, and he slipped the straps of the nightgown from her smoothly rounded shoulders and let the garment fall down to her waist. The full, beautifully cupped breasts were tipped by smoothly pink nipples centered on small, pink circles, and he watched her lips drop open and her eyes lift up to stare past him as he admired the loveliness of her.

His hands took the folds of the nightgown where it had fallen and pushed it lower. She moved her hips and let the garment fall from her entirely to reveal a rounded little belly, sweetly convex, that went into a bushy little triangle of black soft-wire filaments. She rose onto her knees and revealed long, lovely thighs, firm and smooth.

He sat up, reached his lips up, encircled one pink tip, and drew it into his mouth. "Oh . . . oh, God," Annabel breathed, pressing herself against him, pushing more of her breast into his mouth. He caressed, sucked, gently pulled. "Oh . . . ooooh," she moaned, turning onto her back as her arms slid around him. She began to writhe as he kissed her breasts, her body swaying though she lay on her back. Her hands moved up and down his body as though she were painting him, her touch trying to imprint every part of him into her inner being. Small gasping sounds of delight came from her as his lips traced a lambent trail across her breasts, her abdomen, down onto the softly convex little belly. "Oh, oh . . . so good, so good," she groaned.

Her smooth, warm body pressed upward against his as his hand moved down through the black-fiber triangle, pushing down against the domed pubic mound, sliding down farther to touch the wondrous portal. Annabel half-screamed and her body shuddered in ecstasy, but she held her thighs tightly together and his hand kept up a firm pressure as she whirled inside herself. He pressed more and Annabel's hands fluttered up and down his body.

"Kiss me, oh, please, kiss me," she murmured as, her mouth open, she reached out for his lips. He brought his mouth to hers and felt the sucking quivering of her lips as they echoed all the feverish intensity of her body. Slowly, as her mouth held his, her tongue caressing, darting, entreating, her hands moving across his body, he felt her relax her thighs and his hand pressed in deeper at once, cupped the warm, moist portal, and at his touch, Annabel screamed in delight.

Her thighs opened and he probed deeper. Annabel's head tossed from side to side as tiny gasps of delight fell from her lips. Suddenly her hands came against his hips, pulled, and he swung with her, bringing his throbbing, hot maleness against the black floss. He pressed down and waited. Annabel's cry held fear and desire. He felt the wild passion of the flesh and the apprehension of the spirit fighting inside her. He drew back, came forward, and pressed into the warm, wet entrance. Again Annabel cried out, a short, quick gasp and then a wild, long cry of abandon as she threw herself up against him. "Do it, Jesus, do it . . . oh, God, do it," she screamed.

He came forward, sliding smoothly into the moist tunnel, and Annabel cried out in glorious delight. She rose with his every sliding thrust, drawing in all of him, pushing the soft, pliant walls of herself against his pulsating, bulging heat.

He heard the rhythmic gasps begin, each a tiny call of wanting, inner and outer flesh mingling together, joining, blending, that total fusion of spirit and senses, the oneness of ecstasy. Her firm, smooth thighs locked around his waist to hold him hard inside her. She arched her torso backward, the beautifully cupped breasts lifted high, the small pink tips almost quivering, and he saw the glowing loveliness of her as pure sensuous pleasure exploded inside her. He felt the sudden quivering, only a few seconds, before her gasp gathered into a scream and the moment became forever though it lasted only a flash, that instant yet timeless explosion of pure feeling.

"Oh, God, oh God," she murmured as the world began to return and the edge of dismay came into her voice until finally she fell back onto the mattress, a long, shuddered sigh sliding from her. Her arms reached out, circled his neck, and pulled his face down to rest upon the full-cupped breasts, one smooth, pink tip pressing against his eye.

She curved her body into his with a childlike comfortableness.

"Close enough?" Fargo smiled, and she nodded against him.

"I don't know why this happened," Annabel murmured. "I almost can't believe it."

"Does it matter?" Fargo asked.

"It matters," she said. "But right now I can't think of why."

"Go to sleep," he told her, and she murmured agreement with a satisfied sigh. She slept in moments, holding him to her, and he felt his own eyes grow heavy with tiredness. He let sleep sweep over him, his head on the sweet-soft pillows.

6

The morning sun had begun to slide across the campsite when he silently rose, washed with his canteen and dressed, and slipped from the wagon. He settled down against a nearby tree and caught another hour's nap before the camp began to wake; he opened his eyes to see Harriet Crowler's coffeepot on and Humphrey Asgood becoming her first customer. Fargo stayed beside the tree until Annabel emerged clothed in an off-white shirt and blue Levi's, the sun catching the glint of copper in her brown hair. She looked smugly beautiful as she saw him and he rose to go to her.

"Thanks for obeying the proprieties," she said sincerely. "I don't need tongues wagging."

"That should be the most of your problems," Fargo said.

Annabel's eyes swept over the others as they came out for morning coffee. "I'll have to tell them about Terrall," she said.

"You'd best. You've ten guns fewer now," Fargo said. He stayed back as she walked to where the others sipped their coffee. He watched her talk and heard the murmur of surprise and consternation rise into the air when she finished. The murmur became a hum of earnest conversation with David Corry, Asgood, Hodges, and Thomas Turner huddled with

Annabel. Finally, when the hum died down, Fargo drifted over and met Annabel's sober-faced answer.

"We go on," she said, and Fargo's lips tightened.

"I'm sure we'll be fine once we get past the Shoshoni," Avery Osgood said with irritating confidence.

"You won't get past them," Fargo's said. "The Shoshoni live in these mountains. You might get by the ones that have been trailing along with us, but that's all."

"Once we're properly camped and settled in, I'm sure they'll realize we're not a threat," David Corry said.

Fargo made a harsh sound. "A chicken's no threat to a hawk but he gets eaten anyway," he snapped. Turning his back on the others, he strode to the Ovaro, took the hoof pick from his saddlebag, and cleaned the trail crud from the horse's hooves while he let his anger simmer down. They weren't simply stupid, he realized; they were blinded by their own illusions, captives of a dream that refused to allow reality to intrude. He'd find them a place to set up their community as quickly as he could, and be done with them, Fargo told himself. He'd seen the harshness of reality tear apart too many dreams and it was always a grim, searing sight. He could do without another one. He finished with the Ovaro's hooves. As he put his grooming gear away, he saw Annabel come toward him with a wryly quizzical glint in her eyes.

"Seems you forgot to mention everything that happened last night," she said, and he half-shrugged. "I saw Herb Starr having a hard time getting around and asked what had happened. He was limping, aching, and had a bandaged hand."

"He tell you?"

"He told me a bullet had gone through his foot, another had grazed his hip, and still another had hit his hand," she answered. "He didn't add anything more and I didn't ask more. I suppose that's one more thing I have to thank you for."

"For leaving you a carpenter? Yes, that's about right," Fargo said, and pulled himself onto the Ovaro. "Let's roll," he told her as he sent the Ovaro onto the passage that continued to open up northward.

The Trailsman saw the prints of moose, deer, mountain goat and bear as he rode, and he also saw the tracks of the Hostler wagons. They had stayed on the passage as he wandered through the mountain terrain and headed north.

It was a little past noon when he halted at a mountain stream. As the Ovaro drank, Fargo's eyes swept the high peaks in front of him. The Hostler wagons would have to find a way across those peaks to reach their destination, but he had only to find a place for Annabel to settle down and begin to build her community. He made a harsh sound at the thought and his jaw tightened grimly as he scanned the land on all sides.

When the wagons came into sight, he moved on again. The passage grew steeper yet not impassable, and the tracks of the Hostler wagons continued to stay firm in the soil. Not more than a few days old, he estimated as he examined them again. By late afternoon he slowed and watched the wagons roll uphill, the horses plainly tired. He found a spot where the trees fell back from the passage and pulled in to wait. He started to swing down from the saddle but halted as the line of bronzed horsemen appeared on the higher land, materializing wraithlike from the heavily forested terrain. Once again, they simply gazed down, and as Annabel rolled up with the other wagons, they slowly wheeled and vanished into the trees.

Annabel, apprehension wreathing her face, stared up at the now-empty ridge.

Avery Hodges came up along with David Corry. "Are they going to attack?" Hodges asked.

"Dammed if I know. They're sure taking their time about it if they are," Fargo said. "We'll make camp here. Circle your wagons, just to play it safe." He continued to scan the high ridges while the others circled their wagons, and as the day drew to an end, he decided there'd be no attack. The women began to prepare the supper meal, and Fargo, standing outside the circle of wagons, took in the contours of the nearest ridges when he heard the figure approach. He turned to see Vivian coming toward him in the long gray dress, her deep breasts swaying as she moved.

"Didn't have a chance to get to you till now," she said, halting before him. "You took a lot of wind out of Herb's sails, but I'd still watch myself when he recovers."

"I will," Fargo said.

"What you did doesn't change my wanting to leave with you when the time comes," Vivian said, and her arms came around his neck as her lips pressed hungrily against his. "So you don't forget," she murmured before finally stepping back and strolling away as darkness descended.

Fargo stayed a moment longer, watched the darkness enfold the high ridges in its inky embrace, then slowly returned to the circle of wagons, where he took a tin plate of beans and warmed buffalo strips. He ate by himself and had just turned his plate in when Annabel came up with hers and he caught the glare in her quick glance. He strolled after her as she stalked to her wagon, caught up to her before she climbed into the rig.

"What's put a bur under your saddle?" he asked, and she turned angry eyes at him. "You sorry about last night? Mad at yourself?"

"I wasn't, for most of the day," she snapped.

"Go on." Fargo frowned.

"I guess I didn't expect to see Vivian Starr being so grateful to you for shooting up her husband," Annabel said with waspish anger.

He tried a smile that she rejected with a tight-lipped glare. "Vivian was just trying to cover her bets," he said.

Her smile was ice. "She wants to cover and you want to uncover. You'll make a great pair," she snapped, then spun on her heel.

"Guess last night really was a mistake for you," he called after her, and she halted. "You didn't enjoy it."

She looked back at him. "How can you say that?"

"You wouldn't back off so easily if you had," he said with a smile.

"Bastard," she hissed, and strode into the wagon.

Fargo watched her slam the door behind her and strolled between the wagons to stand in the darkness beyond the circled forms as the camp grew still. The moon had come up to outline the contours of the nearby ridges and Fargo's eyes narrowed as he listened for the night sounds of the forest land. But he heard only the strange silence, and he lowered himself onto a log, waited, his ears tuned to the night. The dark continued to remain silent, an almost eerie stillness, and finally he returned to the Ovaro, took the big Sharps from its saddle case, and made his way out of the circle of wagons again.

He began to climb the hillside under the moonlight, using his nose to take in deep drafts of air as he made tracks toward the nearest of the high ridges. But he smelled no fish oil or bear grease, nothing to reveal the Shoshoni nearby. His finger on the trigger of the carbine, he continued to climb until he reached the top of the ridge. He heard the faint scurrying sound of a pair of raccoons, but then raccoons were virtually undauntable creatures, he realized. Other than that, the strange stillness persisted and he sank down on one knee, rested, his finger still resting against the trigger of the Sharps. The half-moon rose high in the sky and he scanned the silhouetted outlines of the other mountain ridges, the deep blackness where the land dropped into valleys. The sound, when it came, was more startling because of the stillness.

The howl exploded suddenly in the night, a lot closer than it had ever been, rising high into the sky, the same howl still unlike any he had ever heard before. He listened to the sound of it hang in the night, rise, fall, rise again, and drift into stillness. The night wind made it seem closer than it really was, he knew, and his eyes swept the distant ridges. Suddenly, on a far high line, he glimpsed a movement, so swift he wasn't really certain he had seen anything. As he wondered whether the night had simply played tricks on his eyes, it came again, with equal suddenness, a bounding form that appeared and disappeared in the same motion. His gaze continued to stay fixed on the distant ridge but nothing moved again.

At last he rose and began to move down the mountainside. It had to have been the wolf that had howled, he told himself, yet he knew he wasn't at all certain. The form had been large, even at that distance, larger than any wolf he had ever seen. Or had the night and the moonlight only made it seem so?

He swore softly and hurried back down the mountainside until he neared the circle of wagons. He halted under an alder, only a dozen feet from the wagons, started to lay out his bedroll when he heard the half-cry, half-scream from Vivian's wagon. He was running toward it when she came out, stumbled, caught herself, and halted against the rear wheel of the wagon. She blinked at him as he reached her, ran one hand across her eyes, and blinked again as she focused on him.

"What happened?" he asked, and she made an effort to straighten up, the heavy breasts pushing against a cotton nightshirt.

"Dream," she muttered.

"Those visions of yours?" Fargo inquired.

"Yes." The woman nodded. "Nightmares, visions, dreams . . . they're all the same. I keep seeing the same thing, everybody dead."

He put a hand on her shoulder and peered hard at her. "You see anything else at all? Think hard, Vivian," he pressed.

She frowned into space, her brow furrowed, her face still chalk-white. "Bodies, pieces of bodies, arms, legs . . . Oh, God," she half-gasped, and clapped her hands to her face. He waited until, with a last shudder, she drew her hands away and met his concerned gaze. "It's all right," Vivian murmured. "It's over. It won't come again tonight, never twice in one night."

He led her back to the wagon, his arm around her waist for support, and as he stepped inside the circle, he saw Annabel looking out from the open tail door of her wagon. "You going to be all right now?"

he asked Vivian, and she nodded. "Where's Herb?" Fargo questioned.

"Asleep inside. He never pays any attention," she said, and her face still drained, she climbed into the big rack-bed rig.

Fargo turned away and met Annabel's disdainful stare. "It's not what you're thinking," he said. "I heard her cry out."

"I did, too," Annabel said. "But I see it was only ecstasy."

"You want your mouth washed out?" Fargo growled. "She had a nightmare."

"In your arms?" Annabel tossed back, each word clothed in sarcasm.

"Asleep in her own wagon, Miss Bitchy," Fargo snapped. "She gets these terrible visions—premonitions, some call them. She told me about them before. She just had one."

Annabel blinked and let the disdain drop from her face. "Premonitions about what?" she asked.

"About our being dead, every last one of us," Fargo snapped out harshly, and saw her apple-cheeked face grow sober.

"You believe in things like that? Premonitions? Visions?" Annabel asked, an edge of apprehension in her voice.

Fargo's chiseled handsomeness didn't soften as he peered back at her. "I believe there's a lot we don't know about in this world." He turned away and started to move between the wagons as he left the circle.

"Fargo," Annabel called out, the word a half-whisper that held its own urgency in it. He halted, looked back at her. She pushed the door of her wagon open further, her hazel eyes dark with inner turbulence. He walked back to her and she retreated into the wagon as he stepped up the tail rung and pushed the door closed behind him, his face still stone.

She came to him as she pushed the shoulder straps of the silk nightgown down and the full-cupped breasts seemed to tumble out at him. "Stay," she whispered as he began to pull off clothes. She came against him as he stood naked before her, his throbbing maleness quickly filling, rising, answering the wanting that emanated from her. He felt himself press into her, just below the convex nap of her pubic mound, and she gasped out. He lay down atop the mattress on the floor of the wagon with her, his warmth still hard against her, and Annabel's lovely thighs fell open at once for him as his mouth found her breast.

"Yes, yes, yes," she murmured while her hands caressed his face, neck, fluttering down across his back to suddenly tighten against him as he touched the already moist portal, held there, waited. "Ah . . . aaaaiii . . ." Annabel half-cried, half-gasped, and pushed her hips upward, her thighs clasping around his legs as she thrust herself onto him, then fell back. She drew him with her. A cry of pure pleasure came from her lips and her neck arched backward.

He slid slowly into her, to the very depths of her, and she gasped out delight that became small purring sounds as she moved slowly back and forth with him, her hips a sinuous messenger of the senses. Annabel's hazel eyes, now dark pools of swimming emotions, stared at him as he made love to her, almost as though she wanted to step outside of herself for still another dimension of pleasure. Her hands came behind his neck, pulled his mouth down to the smooth, soft flesh of the beautifully cupped breasts, and as he gathered one mound into his mouth, he saw her lips part and her neck arch backward.

"Now, oh, God, now . . . oh, oh," Annabel cried, her voice rising. He felt her long thighs tighten against him, her hands dig into his back, and the tightness became all of her warm, soft body. The full-cupped breasts quivered as her inner lips pushed against him. Swept along by the totality of her, he came as she did, the explosion of oneness supreme and devouring, and his groan was almost drowned out by her scream of pleasure. It had been fast, much faster than the last time, but quickness took nothing away from intensity, he found out. When Annabel finally fell back with a deep groan, her arms clasped him around his hips and held him inside her.

"I couldn't hold back," she murmured. "It was as though my body had been just waiting ever since last night. Or maybe seeing you with Vivian set me on fire."

"Nice flame," Fargo commented. "Want to try for another bonfire, only slower this time?"

Her answer was to turn and bring one full-cupped breast to his lips as her hand began to paint a warm path up and down the inside of his thighs. When he made love to her again, it was with slow fire that she answered, everything that had happened with such fast fire happening again but with a smoldering flame. When the final moment erupted, the ecstasy was no different, a fountain of rapture that, no matter what the road traveled to reach, bestowed its own bliss.

She slept at once in his arms when the embers of passion took over, and it wasn't till the first ray of dawn that she woke. He had come awake earlier and lay still beside her as he wrestled with his own thoughts. She rose up on one elbow, one soft pink tip resting against his chest. "What are you thinking?" she asked.

"I'm thinking I'd like to find a way to convince you to hightail out of these damn mountains and give up this damn fool idea," he said, the words harsh but the tone quietly flat.

"You know I can't do that," Annabel answered as she sat up straighter. "We're going to make it work, you wait and see, in spite of Shoshoni and wild premonitions."

"I hope so," he said honestly as he began to pull on clothes.

When he was dressed, she rose, kissed him gently, and her hazel eyes were soft again. "Thanks for being considerate again," she said. "You wait, it'll all turn out fine."

He slipped from the wagon in the early dawn, tossed her a smile, and hurried to where he'd left his bedroll. Perhaps her kind of blithe confidence could make things work, he pondered, but he hated the grimness inside himself that rejected the thought. He gathered his bedroll up and returned it to the Ovaro as Harriet Crowler held a cup of coffee out to him. He took it gratefully, slowly drawing in the bracing brew. The camp was awake and ready to roll when he finished.

Fargo paused to check the cinch under the Ovaro, drew it a fraction tighter, and when he finished, he found Vivian standing by, a sardonic smile on her lips.

"I thought I'd go back to sleep last night but I couldn't," the woman said. "I finally got up and came looking for you. I found your bedroll."

"That's nice," Fargo said carefully.

"You still figure to leave after you find her a place to set up?" Vivian asked with studied casualness.

"Why wouldn't I?"

"Thought maybe you'd had your mind changed."

"No. Annabel knows better. It's never been mentioned."

"It will be," Vivian said confidently.

"No," Fargo said. "Not every woman wants to make a deal, honey."

"Every woman wants," Vivian said simply, and started to turn away. She paused and looked back at him. "None of it changes anything for me. I'm leaving with you." She walked on.

Fargo pulled himself onto the pinto and rode out onto the passage. Annabel's baker's wagon started after him while the others swung into line behind. The passage took a fairly steep turn and Fargo rode slowly and watched the wagons behind. Annabel's wagon was light enough and the horse had little trouble on the grade, but he saw the others struggle and he was glad to see the passage finally level off. He stopped to let the horses rest when the three figures emerged from the trees a dozen yards ahead and rode slowly toward him, the man in the tan stetson leading the other two.

Fargo's hand was on the big Colt as the trio came to a halt. "No trouble, Fargo," the one in the tan hat said, and turned his palms outward. "I'm Simon Crater."

"I know who you are. The other two are Jake and Harry," Fargo growled. "What do you want?"

"To ride with you again," Simon Crater said. "Terrall hired us and we liked the idea of the money, but we never wanted any part of his rough stuff with the girl."

"That's the truth," the one named Jake added.

"I know that," Fargo said, and drew glances of

both surprise and relief from the trio. "Why didn't you keep hightailing it?"

"We figured to do that," the third one said.

"But you're here," Fargo said.

"Truth is we've been plumb scared," Crater said. "Between the Shoshoni all around and the rest of it we've been chewing our nails off."

"What's the rest of it?" Fargo frowned and cast a glance at Annabel, who had rolled to a halt.

"I don't know," Simon Crater said. "We couldn't see anything by night, couldn't hear anything, but we could sure feel something. Jake and Harry will swear to it, too."

Fargo glanced at the other two men, who nodded, their faces tight.

"Something's out there in these damn mountains," Jake said. "Last night we decided to come back here to meet you. We'd feel better riding with you and we figured you could use another three guns."

Fargo glanced at Annabel and she shrugged. "Whatever you say," she told him.

"We can use three more hands," Fargo said, and nodded at the men. "Take your positions with the wagons."

"Much obliged," Simon Crater said, and Fargo saw the relief in the man's face as he spurred his horse on to draw alongside the center wagons. Fargo swung in beside Annabel as he moved the wagons forward.

"The Shoshoni put the fear in them. They're not the kind to get scared about strange things in the night," she said.

"Maybe," he said, and rode on ahead of the wagons.

They stayed with the passage and slowed when it

became a level section of forest land with alders and hackberry thinned out enough to leave the wagons ample room to move through and around them. The Hostler wagons had taken the same way, their wheel marks clear, and Fargo rode still farther on when he saw the trees fall away and the land open into bright sunlight, becoming a kind of high mountain rolling plateau.

It was midday when he found another stream and halted until the others rolled up. As they stopped to let the horses drink, they left the wagons and stretched their own legs. Fargo's eyes swept the group and he saw that Herb Starr still limped considerably but he'd regained almost normal use of his hand. The man's dour expression hadn't changed any, Fargo noted. Avery Hodges and Thomas Turner, the insect expert, manned the supply wagon, he noted, and as he refilled his canteen, he heard the sudden murmur of alarm rise from the others. He looked up to see the Shoshoni who had appeared atop one of the rounded hills across from the wagons.

He rose, strode unhurriedly to the Ovaro as he counted the Indian force. Enough to mount an attack, he decided, and he pulled himself into the saddle. "Everybody stays nice and calm," he called out. "Roll your wagons as though they weren't there." He waited while the others clambered into their rigs and Annabel moved her wagon forward as he rode beside her.

"Shouldn't we be getting ready to make a stand?" she asked.

"I don't think they're going to attack," Fargo said, and frowned up at the Shoshoni. "I can't figure what they're doing, but they seem to come looking to see if we're still around."

"Why?" Annabel questioned, and he shrugged without an answer.

As he moved forward ahead of the wagons, he saw the Indians drift away and disappear behind the top of the hill. He put the Ovaro into a trot and followed the tracks of the Hostler wagons, which had rolled across the gentle hills. Thick forest land lay at the sides of the hills and there seemed ample tree cover on the rolling terrain. This might well be the place to halt and let Annabel and the others set down their community, he mused. The richness of grass and foliage was proof the ground held good water, but he decided to move on farther to see if there might be an even better location. He glanced back and saw the others come into sight.

He sent the pinto on, his eyes sweeping the rolling hills. The Shoshoni had vanished and he was uneasy because of it. But the day was drawing to an end and an attack grew more unlikely. The Shoshoni would sneak-raid by dark but not mount a full-scale attack, he knew. He rode on to where the Hostler wagon tracks crossed a low hill and began to go down into a kind of valley between two low hills.

Fargo rode on, nosed the pinto down into the valley, and felt the furrow crease his brow as he spied the wagons in the distance. They were stopped but in a scattered fashion, strung out with large spaces between each. He put the horse into a canter and hurried down to the floor of the valley. The furrow became a frown as he came into clear sight of the last wagon. It was smashed against a tree, the two wheels on the left broken, some of the contents from inside the wagon spilled onto the ground. He didn't see the four figures until he reached the wagon, heard the gasp come from inside him as he reined to a halt. The bodies were all but decimated, torn apart, most with arms and legs missing, two with heads torn away. Enough clothing remained for him to make out two women and two men. His lips tight, he sent the pinto on to the next wagon.

The horses had broken away and only empty drive shafts remained. Fargo moved the Ovaro slowly around to the other side of the wagon and the curse fell from his lips as he peered at the bodies—six, this time. Once again, not one remained a complete figure, and he saw three other torn forms where they had been dragged a dozen yards from the wagon. He turned and brought his attention back to the wagon and the bodies closest to it, his eyes narrowed in thought. He was about to ride on to the next wagons when he saw Annabel's rig come into sight as she rolled down into the valley, the others in a line close behind her.

His lips thin, he waited a few minutes and then rode to meet the wagons as they drew closer. He raised his hand into the air.

Annabel reined to a halt and nodded into the distance. "Looks as though we've caught up to the Hostler wagons," she said.

"Great," Humphrey Asgood called out. "The stronger we are, the less chance the Shoshoni will attack, I'd imagine."

Fargo backed the Ovaro so he could take in everyone in line. "You'd best take hold of your stomachs. Maybe you'll want to keep the kids inside your wagons," he said, and saw the apprehension flood their faces. "We're going on through. There's no other way," he said, and turned the Ovaro around to swing in beside Annabel."

"They're all dead, aren't they?" she half-whispered.

"I haven't seen them all yet," he said grimly.

"My God," Annabel breathed at his reply.

Fargo heard one of the other wagons pull out of line and turned to see it was David Corry and Avery Hodges on the supply wagon.

"If there's been a massacre, we ought to stop to do the proper thing, Fargo," Hodges said.

"In this country there are a lot of things a man ought to do and damn seldom does," Fargo said.

"I know it's a harsh land and it gets to a man," Hodges insisted with an edge of loftiness to his voice. "But callousness is no excuse for not doing the proper thing."

"Staying alive is," Fargo bit out, and Hodges fell silent.

Fargo slowed when they reached the first wagons, rode to where he had first halted, and watched the others roll to a halt, their eyes wide with shock as they stared at the scene. He saw some of the womenfolk turn away and hold a hand to their stomachs. "Keep going," he said, and rode on to the next three wagons where, the sickness curdling inside his own stomach, he saw what he expected to see; more of the same mutilated, torn bodies. He sat the horse to one side as the others finally rolled up and he saw them gaze with shock and disgust at the scene of carnage.

"Those stinking savages," Fargo heard Seth Crowler mutter, and Bettledorf cursed his agreement.

The Trailsman felt David Corry's eyes on him and he met the man's gaze. "Anything familiar to you about this?" Fargo asked.

"They were torn apart like this at the Frawley wagon," the naturalist said.

"Anything else?" Fargo pressed, and the man shrugged.

"No arrows here, either. Not in any of the wagons and not in any of the bodies."

"You saying the Shoshoni didn't do this?" Seth Crowler asked.

"That's right." Fargo nodded. "No arrows anywhere, no Indian pony tracks near, and nothing taken from the wagons."

"Wolves," Annabel murmured, awe in her voice. "The wolves we've heard at night."

"Could be," Fargo said. "But I've never seen a wolf pack do this kind of job, and we've only heard one wolf howl at night."

"Then, what?"

"Something different," Fargo said. "Whatever it is, wolves or something else, it's not like anything you've ever seen."

"We haven't seen anything but the Shoshoni, not for days, Fargo," Bettledorf said. "It has to be them."

"No," Fargo said firmly. "Something else. I think that's why they've been holding back."

"You mean they're afraid of some wolves?" Annabel frowned.

"Could be, but then I don't think afraid is the word," Fargo said. "There's something more. Fear can be part of it but so can the unwritten codes of the wild. A cougar will back off a prey the grizzly is stalking. A lynx will turn away from a marten on the trail of a kill. Two hawks won't go after the same guinea hen."

"Are you saying the Shoshoni have a pact with a pack of wolves, if that's what they are?" Hodges frowned.

"Not the way you put it, but I'm saying there are codes, understandings, territories, times of dominance. Every creature that is part of the wild—be it man or beast—understands this. It is part of the fabric of their existence in a land where fierceness is its own wisdom," Fargo said. He saw fear behind the frowns that stared back at him.

"No more talk, not here, my God, not here," Harriet Crowler burst out, and flung herself back into her wagon.

"She's right," Fargo said. He moved the pinto on slowly, past the last of the Hostler wagons with its grisly cargo. He glanced back to see the others hurrying after him, and he rode on through the valley while his gaze scanned the silences of the rolling hills.

The terrain began to lift, and he peered ahead to see that the valley most likely came to an end some miles on, but the night approached too quickly. He pulled into a half-moon of land to the right and waved the wagons to a halt. "Pull them into a circle," he ordered as he swung from the horse and surveyed the undulating hills that rose on both sides.

Humphrey Asgood approached him as the women prepared supper. "I'd guess we ought to be setting up sentries tonight," the man said.

"No, not yet," Fargo answered, and the man's jaw fell open. "There'll be no attacking tonight."

"How can you be so blasted sure?" Asgood protested.

"Instincts," Fargo said.

"Damn, that's not an answer that makes me comfortable," Asgood said. He strode away, still muttering.

"Now tell me the real answer," Fargo heard the voice say and turned to see Vivian there.

"The moon." He smiled. "It'll be full in another few nights. If there's going to be a night attack, it'll wait for that."

Vivian came closer just as Annabel stepped between the wagons. "Oh, sorry," Annabel said at once, her face tightening. "I didn't know I was interrupting anything." She started to spin and halted at Vivian's voice.

"You're being stupid. You didn't interrupt anything," Vivian said. "I'm too terrified to get laid." She turned to Fargo, her eyes deep, sudden lines in her face. "The Hostler wagons, that's how I saw things in my premonitions, exactly like that."

Annabel stepped closer. "Maybe that's what you've been seeing all along in your dreams," she said. "You just assumed it was us, but it really was the Hostler wagons."

"No, I saw us. I saw Herb and the Crowlers, everybody all torn apart," Vivian insisted and trembled.

Fargo's hands held her shoulders until the trembling stopped. "You can't be sure, not about any of it," he told her. "Go to sleep, rest even if you don't sleep." She nodded and returned to her wagon and he tossed a glance at Annabel. "You, too," he growled.

"What are you going to do?" she asked.

"Put it all in order. There are things that connect," Fargo said. "That little girl from the Frawley wagon saw something so terrible she won't give voice to it. The old prospector died of a heart attack in that tree, but his eyes stared with the same unholy terror I saw in that little girl's eyes. Now there's the Hostler wagons, the same as the Frawley wagon. It hangs together."

"And now?" she asked.

"We wait for morning," he said. "Go to sleep."

She left, going silently into the wagon and closing the door behind her.

Fargo settled down beside a tree trunk that let him see the low hills beyond the wagons. He expected the howl to pierce the night but there was only silence and he finally let himself fall asleep, one hand on the butt of the Colt at his hip.

When morning came, he woke to a bright sun, his eyes automatically going to the low hills on all sides. But nothing moved and he stepped inside the circle of wagons to the Ovaro, used his canteen to wash, and watched the others emerge from their rigs. One of the women made coffee and he took a cup as Annabel came over to him. "Sleep well?" he asked.

"Hardly," she muttered. He tilted his head back, drained the last of the coffee, and when he brought his head down, his eyes went to the near hills. Annabel, obviously seeing his jaw muscles tighten, quickly moved to follow his gaze and he heard the tiny gasp from her lips. The five shapes had appeared suddenly, along the side of the hill, unmistakably wolves yet ordinary enough.

Fargo saw Avery Hodges halt and spot the animals and in moments everyone in the camp had their eyes on the hills. Fargo caught the movement to his right and saw the second group of brown-gray forms appear. Five more, he counted when atop a hill to his left a line of slowly moving forms materialized. The wolves formed a straight line as they walked and suddenly came to a halt and settled down on their haunches facing the wagons below.

"Ten more," Fargo muttered aloud.

"Christ, over there," Simon Crater swore, and Fargo's glance snapped to the top of another low hill where at least ten more thick-furred forms were grouped.

"My God, on this side," he heard one of the women gasp, and he spun to gaze up at the hill on the other side of the wagons. Two more groups of wolves looked down from the top of a low hill, some twenty in all, he counted quickly, and suddenly, wherever he looked, there were more knots of wolves.

"There's got to be seventy of them," he murmured.

"I've never heard of more than twenty in a pack," Avery Hodges said. "This is a-a—"

"An army," Fargo finished for him. "And there's one more to come." He had just said the words when the form bounded into view on the center ridge and Fargo stared at the largest, most magnificently powerful wolf he had ever seen. Pure white, except for ink-black nose and deep dark eyes, the wolf looked down at the wagons below with a long, steady stare. He weighed at least a hundred and fifty, Fargo guessed, his legs straight and powerful, loins sloping down into a croup made for tireless running, shoulders thick with powerfully bunched muscles. The white wolf turned his head first one way, then the other, surveying his vast pack before bringing his gaze back to the wagons. Slowly, he lifted his head and the deep, commanding howl rose from his throat, a pronouncement and a challenge, a warning and a promise.

"You don't have to wonder anymore about what happened to the other wagons or the old prospector," Fargo said.

"My God, we can never fight off all of them," Harriet Crowler said.

"Maybe not, but life's suddenly gotten simpler. You've no choice but to fight," Fargo said. He surveyed the mass of silent forms that dotted the hillsides. Some were mostly gray, a few almost black, some mostly brown, but most were a gray-brown intermix. All were powerful examples of northern timber wolves. Except for their pure white leader, Fargo grunted. He was an arctic wolf that had somehow worked his way south, his coat thicker than the others', his face broader at the cheeks. He had fashioned not a wolf pack that foraged for food but an avenging army, disciplined and fierce. Fargo saw the white wolf's eyes staring back at him, pools of simmering hate. "Get your wagons. Time to move," Fargo said.

"What if they attack suddenly?" one of the women asked.

"They won't. Not yet. They'll wait and watch some more, I hope long enough for us to find a better place to make a stand," he said as he climbed onto the Ovaro. He rode a few paces in front of Annabel as he led the train forward. He saw the great white wolf move along with him while the others began to drift away behind. As the white wolf moved along with him high on the ridge, Fargo cast only an occasional glance his way. They had gone on for more than an hour when he heard Annabel's question, fear and alarm in her voice.

"Why is he doing that? He keeps watching you," she asked, and Fargo slowed the Ovaro and came abreast of her. A grim smile edged his lips, touched with admiration.

"He's making sure I'm your leader," he said. "He's sizing me up. You could say he's watching to see what I'm watching. That's the way of the wolf, and this one is no ordinary pack leader."

"Why us, why only wagon trains and old prospectors? Why not the Shoshoni?" Annabel asked. "I know, you said there's a code, an understanding."

"And more. We're the intruders here in these

mountains. Everything else belongs here," Fargo said. He put the Ovaro into a trot as he rode on ahead of the wagons. The end of the valley lay directly ahead and the land rose again to become one, rolling level. But the trail held, and when Fargo took the wagons from the valley, the wolves were almost on the same level. But they kept plenty of distance and Fargo continued to ride on until, near the noon hour, he spotted a strong mountain stream that crossed their path, and he waved the wagons to a halt.

He swung to the ground, let the Ovaro drink, and refilled his canteen. The wolves had drawn back still deeper into the trees and were for the most part impossible to see now. The others cast nervous glances his way as they halted.

"How can you stop for this? How can you be so dammed casual?" David Corry burst out, his words echoing everyone else's thoughts.

"You show fear and you'll be dead a lot quicker." Fargo smiled. "They're watching us, as they have for days. They're waiting for us to do something that'll help them."

"I think it's time to open the supply wagon and start handing out the extra rifles and all the extra boxes of ammunition we have there. We can bring out those two cases of gunpowder we have there, too," Avery Hodges said.

"No," Fargo snapped out sharply. "Leave the supply wagon alone."

"I agree with Avery. We ought to start unpacking. It'll take a while to get everything unpacked and handed out," David Corry protested.

"Leave the supply wagon alone. Right now it's just another wagon to them and I want it to stay that way." Fargo frowned.

"Aren't you giving them a little too much credit, Fargo?" Hodges half-sneered. "I've studied wolf behavior."

"Out of books?" Fargo tossed back and Hodges' face reddened. "Drive the supply wagon just as usual," the Trailsman said. "I'm going to ride on ahead. I might be a couple of hours. You just keep moving along this trail."

"I don't like this, Fargo, not any part of it," Hodges insisted, but Fargo ignored the man, turned the Ovaro, and set off at a fast canter. He kept the fast pace, cast a glance to his left, and saw the white wolf come into sight, keeping pace with a long, loping stride. Just to prove to himself what he was all but certain of, Fargo drew the big Sharps from the rifle case and swerved the pinto directly toward the white form. The wolf halted, moved at an angle into the trees, and vanished from sight. The wolf was not about to risk being picked off.

Fargo uttered a grunt of bitter admiration. His foe was cunning, wily, and intent on following his own plan. He wouldn't change it, Fargo knew, unless some unexpected opportunity presented itself. Fargo swerved back onto the rough trail and continued on, his eyes sweeping the land ahead as he sought terrain that would give them half a chance of surviving. He frowned suddenly as the rough trail grew harsher and the terrain turned rocky and cut through with ravines, draws, rock-bound box canyons, and a network of narrow trails. The trail he rode suddenly edged a ravine on one side, not terribly deep but deep enough to demolish a wagon that went over the edge and into it. The trail was wide enough for the wagons single-file, he took note, and at the other end of the ravine it widened again. There he saw at least two box canyons and an area framed by high rock slabs on three sides.

It offered as good a spot to make a stand as any he had seen. He turned the Ovaro and started back to meet the wagons, riding hard along the narrowed section that bordered the ravine. When he left the ravine, he put the pinto into a gallop and rode hard, but his eyes swept the trees on all sides. He saw no white furred form watching. The wolf had broken off his watchful pursuit to return to the others. Fargo saw the sun sliding into the midafternoon sky when he came in sight of the wagons.

As he saw the wagons, he also saw the woods to the right move with gray-brown stealthy forms that appeared and disappeared like so many shadows. He reined to a halt and let the wagons come up to him. "I expected I'd be meeting you before this," Fargo said to Annabel, and saw her lips tighten.

"We stopped for a spell," she murmured, and met his frown. "Avery and David insisted," she added, and Fargo moved the pinto down the line of wagons. The three naturalists stepped from their wagons along with the Hardings, Bettledorf, and another couple.

"I won't mince words about it, Fargo," Avery Hodges said. "I didn't like the idea of your riding off on your own."

"Avery said you could be running out on us, taking the opportunity to save your own skin and literally throw us to the wolves. He wouldn't listen to me," Annabel said.

"I'll admit it. That's what I felt," the man said. "So I insisted we take a vote. It was close but I won."

"A vote on what?" Fargo queried, his brow furrowing.

"On starting to unpack the supply wagon," Hodges said. "We stopped and got a start on it, handed out all the extra rifles. We figure to get out all the extra ammunition tonight after we make camp."

Fargo's face darkened as he stared at the man. "You stopped, opened the supply wagon, took out the extra rifles, and handed them out," he said.

"Exactly," David Corry said. "I voted along with Avery. It seemed the prudent thing to get a start on preparing."

"You fools. You stupid-ass fools," Fargo spit out. "All you did was get a start on preparing to die."

7

Both men glared back at him. "Rubbish," Avery Hodges threw back. "You're giving them more credit than they deserve. You'd still like us to turn back."

"It's too late for that now," Fargo said. "After your boneheaded play I'm wondering if it's too late to go forward."

"You really think they'll know this is a special wagon just because we took all the extra rifles from it?" Hodges said disdainfully. "Isn't that stretching things? They're simple predators and they attack when they're ready."

"The wolf is the smartest of all predators. Like men, they observe, reason, conclude, and then work together. All predators on the trail will pick out a weak animal or a young one and go after it. A wolf pack, especially with a great leader, will do a lot more than that," Fargo said. "They'll watch how the prey travels, what it does when it slows, when it loses concentration, or if it stays alert. More important, a wolf pack doesn't just concentrate on its prey the way a mountain lion does. If there's a herd, it'll watch the rest of the animals just as carefully and see how protective they are. They'll make sure to pick out the leader and see how alert and watchful he is, and they'll try to see what makes the herd come together and what makes it scatter. They don't just trail, they study behavior. I know two old trappers who swear that wolves use the flight patterns of hawks and even crows to find prey."

He halted, swept the two men with a look of disgust, and turned away to meet Annabel's eyes.

"Do we go on?" she asked.

"We have to," he said grimly. "This is no place to make a stand." His eyes went past her to the trees and he saw the pure white form standing silently, waiting, watching, the others of his huge pack spaced in small groups throughout the forest terrain. "We're going to move fast," he said. "Single-file, no stops."

Simon Crater, Jake, and Harry brought their horses to him. "You want us to ride shotgun next to the supply wagon?" Simon asked.

Fargo's lips pulled back in a grimace as he considered the suggestion. "No," he decided. "If I'm wrong, if they didn't pick up on it, putting extra riders around it will surely mark it for them. Just stay a little closer than usual to it."

Simon nodded and Fargo put the Ovaro into a fast trot. He saw Annabel snap the reins hard over her team and the horses respond at once. He led the way forward and watched the woods seem to move with gray-brown forms that kept silent pace. The white wolf had raced ahead, he saw, a pale form moving swiftly in and out of the trees. Fargo rode on and suddenly glimpsed the wolf peering down at him from a rock ledge as he passed beneath it. The great wolf's mouth hung open as he panted from his burst of speed. Fargo took in the gleaming white fangs, at least two inches in length. He also felt the Ovaro grow uneasy under him, the horse very much aware of the wolf's presence. He stroked the pinto's smooth, warm neck soothingly with one hand as he spurred the horse on.

He slowed some to keep in sight of the wagons as they raced behind him, but another hour passed and the last of the day began to fade when he reached the narrow section of trail alongside the ravine. He halted and saw Annabel and the others slow, fear flooding their faces when they saw the ravine.

"It's wide enough," he called out. "Stay hard against the left side. Keep going and don't look back and don't stop, no matter what you might hear behind you." He drew the Ovaro to one side, motioned Crater, Jake, and Harry over to him, and sent the wagons forward.

Annabel, first in line, rolled onto the narrow section of the trail with room to spare. The Crowlers' rack-bed behind her was a tighter fit, but there was enough room if no one swerved, he saw. His eyes went to the trees where he saw the white wolf standing half atop a fallen log, peering down, and behind him the small sea of gray-brown forms moved restlessly.

"They didn't make a move against the supply wagon," Crater said. "Seems you guessed wrong."

"Seems so." Fargo frowned, his eyes still on the white wolf.

Bettledorf's wagon was next to the last in line, and as it swung onto the narrow length of trail, Fargo motioned to Crater and the other two men to follow him as he swung in just ahead of Hodges and David Corry on the supply wagon. He glanced back, watched Hodges send the supply wagon onto the narrow ledge, and heard the curse fall from his lips as the sound tore the dusk in two. The white wolf's howl rose with a powerful, commanding roar, no bay but a clarion call to action.

Fargo saw a dozen gray-brown forms streak from the trees and onto the narrow trail. They caught up to the wagon in moments, and while Hodges desperately clung to the reins, David Corry drew a six-gun and tried to bring down the racing forms. But the wolves raced tight alongside the wagon and two nimbly leapt between the wheels to race underneath, and the man emptied his gun without hitting a single target. Fargo drew his Colt and fired as he raced on and found the flashing dark forms almost impossible to hit.

The three riders alongside him did no better, he saw. He cursed as he spotted four racing forms squeeze between the rocky wall at one side and the front wheels of the wagon. Two leapt upward, jaws snapping at the front shoulders of the nearest horse, while the other two sank fangs into its hindquarters. He heard the horse scream in pain, but even if it hadn't been bitten, both horses were in panic. The horse veered sharply to its right in an effort to escape the attack, carrying the horse next to him along, and Fargo saw Hodges lose control of the reins. It took only seconds for horses and wagon to plunge off the edge of the trail and into the ravine. Fargo, almost at the other end of the narrow section, reined to a halt and cursed as he emptied his Colt at the six wolves that had begun to streak back along the ledge. When he finished, five lay dead, and in the twilight at the other end of the ravine, he saw the white form standing quietly, gazing back at him with a cold and deadly promise.

Fargo turned the Ovaro and rode on to where the others had halted. They stared down at the bottom of the ravine, faces wreathed in shock and horror.

It was Thomas Turner, the expert on insects, whose voice broke the silence with a hoarse whisper.

"My God, you were right," he breathed. "They marked the wagon."

"Astounding," Annabel murmured.

"Not if you know wolves," Fargo said. He gestured to where the three tall slabs of rock formed a three-way wall behind a cleared space. "Over there," he said, "backs to the stones, wagons in a half-circle in front of you." They followed him quickly and were camped as the last of the daylight faded away. A small fire offered enough light and warmth for the supper meal, though he noticed that no one did more than pick at their food.

"What, now, Fargo?" Bettledorf asked. "We just wait?"

"Can't afford to do that. Thanks to our two departed wolf experts, you have all the extra rifles without the ammunition you'll need. I've got to try to get that ammunition and whatever else I can bring," Fargo said.

"You mean go down into the ravine?" Harding asked.

"Yes, I can go down from this end, but it won't be that simple. I'll bet they've already sent at least two or three of the pack down there for the night," Fargo said.

"You mean to guard it?" someone else asked incredulously.

"Partly that. They look on it as their kill now. But they know it was important to us and we might try to get it back, more or less," Fargo said.

"Which is just what you want to try," Annabel said.

"I've no choice. We're going to need every bit of that ammunition to have any kind of a chance," Fargo said.

"You won't have a chance if they're down there waiting," Annabel said.

"I'm working on that," Fargo told her. "Meanwhile, get me two burlap sacks. You ought to have some with you."

"I've some. I'll get them," Lucy Harding said, and hurried to her wagon. Fargo stepped between the wagons and halted at the other side, where he looked down into the ravine. The almost full moon revealed a good tree growth along the sides and mostly scrub and rock at the bottom. The wagon was only a dim bulk in the distance. He let thoughts revolve in his mind until he finally returned inside the half-circle of wagons. The wolf pack had crossed the narrow trail to this side by now, he knew, but they'd wait till tomorrow night for the full moon to launch an all-out attack. There was time to prepare for that. Not much time, but enough. First things first, and that meant retrieving the ammunition they'd need for any sort of a chance.

Lucy Harding saw him and approached with the two burlap sacks. Annabel hurried after her and he saw the others gather. "There'll be no sneaking up on them, not with their noses and their ears," he said. "Which means we outfox them. Crater, you, Jake, and Harry get your horses. I'll need one more person with me to help carry stuff."

"I'll go," Annabel said, her voice almost drowned out by Vivian's. Both women paused, glanced at each other and then back to him.

"Toss a coin," he grunted. "I'll get one of the extra horses." He hurried to the last wagon, untied one of the spare horses, and when he returned, Vivian had moved a pace closer.

"First time I ever won anything," she said.

"Could be the last time," he told her.

"No matter." She shrugged. "I don't like waiting around for anything, especially to be killed."

Fargo turned the horse over to her and took the Ovaro's reins as she climbed onto the saddle.

"What if they attack while you're down there?" Annabel asked quietly.

"I'm betting against that," he said.

"Besides the boxes of ammunition, there's a small keg of gunpowder and eight sticks of dynamite. We thought we might need it," she said. "I'm surprised it didn't explode when the wagon hit."

"Dynamite does funny things. Sometimes it goes off at anything and other times it takes a lighted fuse," he said as he pulled himself onto the pinto.

Her hand reached out to cover his. "Good luck," she murmured, her hazel eyes grave.

He nodded back, swung onto the pinto, and led the others out between the wagons.

"Let's say there's from four to six of them down by the wagon," Fargo said as he began to move down the slope into the ravine. "We'll ride in as though we don't expect them there. They'll attack and we run. Even with the moon, it'll be dark and there's a lot of high brush. While we're running, Vivian and I will hit the ground. You take my horse, Crater, somebody else takes hers. If we do it right, they won't know we slipped off and keep after you."

"And after you leave us?" Crater asked.

"You let them run you up and down through the high brush for a while, but not too long. Then you hightail it back out of the ravine with all the horses and back to the wagons," Fargo instructed.

"While they're running us you'll be getting the ammo." Crater nodded.

"That's the plan. We ought to have it all and some distance on us by the time they go back to the wagon.

We'll be crawling our way out of the ravine, so don't expect us soon," Fargo said. He glanced at Vivian to see if she'd taken in everything and saw her nod to him. He tossed one of the sacks to her. "Take that with you when we jump," he said.

He brought his eyes to the terrain ahead as they reached the bottom of the ravine. He steered the Ovaro through high brush along the sides of the ravine bottom, which turned out to be narrower than it appeared from above. The broken form of the wagon came into view, shattered into four pieces. Fargo rode directly toward it and drew within a dozen yards before the furred forms appeared, eyes a baleful amber caught by the moonlight. His guess had been wrong by one, he saw as he counted seven wolves. They came forward with low snarls, immediately separating into two groups to form a barrier in front of the wagon.

Fargo swerved the Ovaro to the left and sent the horse thundering into the high brush as Vivian rode beside him and the three men at his heels. He saw the wolves go after them and motioned for Crater and the other two men to crowd in around him. A cluster of low dwarf maples loomed ahead, their branches shutting out most of the moonlight, and he sent the horses racing toward them. The wolves had almost caught up to them, content to fan out on both sides of fleeing horses.

"Ready?" he hissed at Vivian, and she nodded. The Ovaro thundered into the low-branched maples and the high brush and with a quick glance he saw the following wolves increase speed to stay within range of the galloping horses. He slowed the Ovaro, saw Vivian slow with him. Crater, Jake, and Harry came abreast of them. "Now," Fargo snapped out and leapt from the horse as he tossed the reins to

Crater. Fargo hit the ground and lay facedown as the horses thundered past him. He stayed motionless until the horses had raced on a dozen yards, then he raised his head and saw the strung-out tails of the wolves giving chase. He looked to his side to see Vivian pushing herself up from the ground.

"Let's go," he muttered. "Every second counts."

She was beside him instantly as he ran for the remains of the wagon. He could hear the horses thundering through the brush, moving down the length of the ravine. They'd be heading back all too soon, he knew as he ripped pieces of the canvas away from the wagon. The ammunition boxes were easy enough to find, and he began stuffing them into his sack. "Take as many as you can carry," he said to Vivian, and she clambered across the broken frame of the wagon, flinging more of the boxes into the sack she dragged along. Fargo rummaged through the debris surrounding the wagon, kicked away rakes and hoes and shovels that would never be used again.

"I've all the ammunition boxes I can find," Vivian called, and Fargo cursed as he heard the horses galloping back. He flung aside a cluster of saws tied together and saw the small keg of gunpowder. He clawed at it, scooped it into his sack, and spied the eight sticks of dynamite. They were banded together in a protective bundle of straw and he shoved them into the sack, rose, and started running with Vivian beside him. He heard the horses drawing closer, risked going on another twenty yards and then fell flat, pulling the woman with him.

Hardly breathing, he listened to the horses race by, the wolves keeping pace with them. He heard Crater lead the way to the other end of the ravine and start to climb upward. He rose, yanked at Vivian, and she came with him. He ran again in a crouching lope and Vivian managed to stay only a few paces behind. When he heard the horses racing up the end of the ravine, he turned left, swept the ground with a piercing glance, and beckoned the woman toward a cluster of mountain brush.

She was at his side as he hit the ground and wriggled into the brush. "The wolves will be coming back to the wagon now," he said. "I just hope we're far enough away so they won't pick up our smell." She lay still beside him and he strained his ears and picked up the soft scrape of bodies moving through the brush and the faint sound of panting mouths. He followed their path with his ears, heard them half-circle as they returned to the wagons. Finally the sounds died away and he pressed Vivian's arm as he began to crawl forward. She moved with him, at a slow, steady pace, and he finally felt the ground begin to rise. He started to crawl upward with Vivian pressed against him when he froze and his nostrils flared. The scent drifted to him, the odor unmistakable. He kept one hand on Vivian's head, holding her flat to the ground as he carefully raised his own face and peered back the way they had crawled. It took him a few moments before he spied the dark form moving back and forth across the ground, long snout held down every few moments to sniff.

Fargo's eyes peered beyond the wolf, swept the moonlit brush and intermittent tree cover. But there was no other four-legged hunter and he lifted his hand from Vivian's head. "One of them halfway caught our trail," Fargo murmured. "He's trying to nail it down."

"How'd you know he was there?"

"I've an educated nose, too," Fargo muttered. "But he's alone. I've got to take care of him without any of his friends knowing about it. That means no shooting." He reached down to the narrow leather holster around his calf and drew out the thin, double-edged throwing knife, as perfectly balanced as it was sharp. "I'm going to make you the bait," he whispered, and Vivian frowned. "I can't risk him coming at me and dodging. If I miss, he'll let out a roar and the rest will come charging. When I motion, you get up and start running."

Fargo rolled from her, rolled again until he was a good fifteen feet away. His eyes went to the wolf in time to see the animal stiffen, lift its head, and sniff the air. The Trailsman motioned to Vivian and she pushed to her feet, the sack in one hand, and began to run toward the end of the ravine. Fargo saw the wolf spring forward at once, flattening its body as it streaked across the ground after the fleeing figure. It would only take a few seconds for the wolf to reach her, Fargo knew, and he followed the animal's all-out charge. He measured distance, angle, drew his arm back, and sent the throwing knife hurtling through the air. The needle-pointed blade struck the charging wolf through the side of his neck, just below the powerful jaw muscles. It embedded itself to the hilt through the thick fur.

Fargo rose, following the wolf as it broke its charge, twisted, fell, and twisted again. With a final burst of effort, the wolf tried to regain its feet once more but succeeded only in falling on its side with a final death quiver.

Fargo drew a deep breath as he retrieved the throwing knife, cleaned it off, and pushed it back into the calf holster. Vivian had come to a halt and he caught up to her in moments. "We walk from here," he said. "Fast." She stayed with him, he saw in admiration, and he slowed his pace as he saw her breath come in harsh gasps. When they reached the top of the ravine, she dropped to the ground and he knelt beside her as she regained her breath.

"We did it," she murmured. "You did it, really. It was all your show."

"You were there," he said. He lifted her to her feet and they walked arm and arm back to the wagons. Most of the others woke when they arrived, Annabel the first out of her wagon as he emptied the sacks on the ground.

"Keep the gunpowder and the dynamite in your wagon," Fargo told her. "The rest of you divide up all the extra ammunition. Now I'm going to get some shut-eye."

After checking where Crater had put the Ovaro, Fargo took his bedroll down and stretched out at the edge of the half-circle of wagons, almost underneath the Crowlers' big rack-bed. He drew sleep around himself at once, aware that the new day would come all too soon.

When morning came and he slowly rose and dressed, the plans in his mind had already sorted themselves out. It didn't take that much sorting, he grimaced inwardly. There were few options and he gratefully sipped the cup of coffee Lucy Harding handed him. He stepped to a space between two of the wagons and gazed out across the clear area.

The brown-gray forms were gathered on the hillside, some lying down, others seated, all silent and alone, at the bottom of the hill. The great white wolf sat on its haunches and gazed across the open space at the wagons. Fargo stepped out past the wagons, into the clear, halted, and faced the white form. Bitterness tinged his smile as the wolf rose up on its feet, the gesture a sign of recognition. The wolfpack leader peered at him with its dark, almond-shaped eyes and finally, with almost deliberate disdain, turned his back and slowly climbed onto the hillside with the others.

"Too many, Fargo," he heard the voice murmur behind him and turned to see Annabel there. She had echoed the thought that burned inside him, but he didn't tell her so.

"Maybe," he allowed. "But maybe not. Maybe we can hurt them enough to make them give up the idea." He returned to the half-circle inside the line of wagons and found everyone waiting, their eyes searching his face for a sign of hope. "There'll be no mystery about the basics of it," he began. "Not for us and not for them. They'll come straight at us. It's the only way they have with those stone slabs surrounding us on three sides. They know we'll be waiting to meet the attack. They're figuring to just overrun us."

"Seems to me that's just what they'll do," Herb Starr put in bitterly.

"If we try just ordinary shooting at them," Fargo said. "But we're not going to do that. You'll be under the wagons. Those on the right will fire to the left, those on the left to the right."

"We set up a cross fire," Simon Crater said.

"That's right. Those in the center will fire straight ahead," Fargo said. "I'll take two men and stay back. Our job will be to bring down any of those who do get through. We'll go through some dry runs, starting now. I want everybody to know exactly what they're going to be doing."

With a murmur of renewed hope, they followed him to the half-circle of wagons, where he spent most of the day drilling them on what to expect, how to stay steady, and most important, the kind of cross fire they'd have to lay down.

"Don't take aim. Don't try to pick and shoot. They'll be coming too fast for that," he instructed. "You just keep shooting at the shapes that'll be charging in front of you. In a good cross fire somebody else's shot will get the ones you miss. With the extra rifles, we've four guns per person. That means you won't have to stop to reload each time. You empty one gun, you pick up another one beside you."

"What about the youngsters, Fargo?" Lucy Harding asked. "Most of them are old enough to shoot."

"There are six of them, as I count. They'll keep reloading rifles," he said. "They'll move up and down the wagons and reload as they go. They can start practicing that right now." He stepped back and watched the youngsters jump at their tasks with the enthusiasm that only the very young could command. It turned the grimness of reality into a kind of game that was its own armor, and finally the dusk began to slide across the land. All the drills had been done with, everyone knew what they were to do.

Lucy Harding had made coffee and some sourdough biscuits. No one had an appetite for more, and as darkness fell, Fargo leaned against the center wagon.

Vivian paused at his side. "No dreams anymore. No premonitions. The real thing now," she said with an edge of wryness.

"Maybe the real thing will be very different," he told her.

Her smile stayed as she brought her lips to his, her deep, soft breasts warm against him for a long moment. Finally she pulled away. "I'm glad there was you," she murmured, then hurried away.

Fargo stayed beside the wagon, and when he saw

the moon appear over the nearest mountain peak, he called out softly. "Take your positions," he said, and the others immediately began to move beneath the wagons. "Jake and Harry, you'll stay with me as backup," he said. The two men nodded gravely.

The Trailsman walked the inside perimeter of the wagons and saw that each person had the extra rifles on hand, the boxes of ammunition in place. He glanced at the youngsters who were crouched at both ends of the half-circle. He knelt down on one knee and peered out from beneath the wagons as the moonlight grew brighter. His gaze fixed on the dark outline of the hill at the end of the clear land, he waited, and the minutes seemed to drag on as though they were hours when suddenly he saw the night move, the pale light of the moon picking up the mass of slowly loping forms that came toward him.

They took shape, became thick-furred bodies of ghostly brown under the pale light, and they stretched from one end of the clear land to the other. The great white wolf was not among them, Fargo saw, and he grunted grimly. The pack leader was hanging back, ready to direct his fanged army.

Fargo watched the wolves draw closer in their slow, loping walk, and suddenly the powerful howl rent the night and the loping walk became a full-strided run. They were into their charge instantly and Fargo held fire, waited, let them come still closer, and finally sent his own command into the night.

"Fire!" he shouted. He rose to his feet and began to run back to where Harry and Jake waited. The furious fusillade of rifle fire echoed from the rock slabs and he heard the sounds of snarls and high-pitched yelps of pain mingle in with the staccato bombardment. He drew back some thirty feet from the wagons with Jake and Harry and dropped to one knee, again facing the wagons. "That's it, that's it," he shouted as he heard the gunfire continue to hold steady when two dark forms came into view as they leapt atop the center wagon. He raised the big Sharps and fired and one of the wolves pitched lifelessly from atop the wagon. Jake and Harry combined to bring down the other. Two more wolves got through, this time near the end of the wagons, one hurtling in between two rack-beds. Fargo's shot turned it twisting in midair before it hit the ground.

Others were getting through but he expected that, and with Jake and Harry he had no trouble dropping each of them at once. Suddenly he heard the gunfire die away. "They're turning, running," he heard Bettledorf call.

"Get everything reloaded," Fargo said. "That was only the first charge." He stayed in place, the two men flanking him, and not more than two or three minutes had gone by when he heard the tightness in Bettledorf's voice.

"Here they come again," the man said.

"Keep the cross fire going," Fargo said. The rifles began firing almost at once. "Damn," he bit out. They were being anxious, wasting bullets by firing too soon. But he soon heard the snarls and screams of pain again, and this time four big, furred shapes crashed through the fusillade to leap onto the wagons and in between them. He fired, brought down two, saw Jake and Harry get the other two when another four crashed through. Once again the big Sharps rang out and two of the wolves somersaulted in midair.

"Over there," Fargo shouted, and Harry and Jake spun with him as three attackers squeezed in between the last wagon and the rocks. As he fired, two more came through, and he ran forward as he fired, Jake and Harry behind him. "Keep pouring it in there. Let them see they can't get through that way," he shouted. One of the wolves spun, flattened himself, avoided two bullets, and charged directly at him. Fargo dropped down, aimed, and fired; the wolf twisted, turned half onto its back, and landed not more than three feet from him.

Harry and Jake were still pouring fire into the opening at the end of the wagons when the gunfire broke off again.

"They're running," someone shouted.

Fargo rose and hurried to the wagons and sank to the ground beside Annabel and Seth Crowler to see the gray-brown forms recede into the darkness.

"We got a lot of them, dammit," Seth said excitedly. "There's got to be at least twenty dead ones out there."

"We got ten that broke through," Fargo heard Harry add triumphantly.

"That leaves forty to fifty," Fargo bit out grimly.

"I think maybe they've had enough," Bettledorf said.

Fargo saw Annabel's eyes on him and he turned away and pushed to his feet. The furious cross fire used up a lot of ammunition, but it was the only thing that had held the pack at bay this far. "How much extra ammunition is left?" he asked as he walked along the edge of the wagons.

"About two boxes for each person," one of the youngsters answered.

Fargo frowned as he made a fast calculation in his mind. "Enough for one more charge, maybe two," he muttered.

"Hell, another two charges like these and we'll have 'em finished off," Seth Crowler said.

Fargo turned away again. The man's mathematics was wrong. The white wolf would still be left with at least a dozen in his pack, perhaps a few more. Without ammunition, it'd be rifle butts against fangs, Fargo grimaced. Yet it was perhaps the best end to it that could be achieved. The question was whether the wolf leader would be willing to sacrifice almost all of his fanged army for this single victory. He was too cunning for that, Fargo decided. The white wolf would not decimate his great force, nor would he simply give up. Fargo peered out across the cleared space with the deep grimness still inside him.

The ground a dozen yards from the wagons was littered with brown forms, scattered from one side to the other, and Fargo turned away, his brow furrowed, when he heard Seth Crowler's cry. "Here they come again," the man called out, and Fargo dropped to one knee to peer out beneath the wagons. The wolves were charging, moving with full force.

"Prepare to fire," he said as he rose, and retreated to take up the backup position with Jake and Harry. The furious fusillade of gunfire erupted just as Fargo heard the white wolf's voice, a sharp, staccato, barklike sound in the distance. The cross fire continued but suddenly petered out. "What is it?" he called.

"Most of 'em turned and ran," Harding answered, and Fargo ran to the wagons to drop down beside Annabel again. He saw sudden movement amid the brown forms that littered the ground and everyone began firing at once, pouring bullets into the furred targets.

"Damn," Fargo swore aloud. "Hold your fire." the gunfire broke off and Fargo heard the white wolf's cry rise into the air, a short, vibrating call. Almost as one, over half the gray-brown forms leapt up and streaked back to the hill, out of range before any of the others managed to get a round off.

"They charged and the first rows fell down alongside the dead ones while the others broke off and ran," Seth Crowler said.

"And you kept firing at them," Fargo said.

"That's right." The man nodded and a murmur of agreement rose from the others.

"But most of your bullets were going into the ones you'd already killed," Fargo said, and he looked down at the ammunition boxes. "And you used up over half the ammunition left and got maybe another four wolves." He stepped back and a grim sound fell from his lips. It wasn't their fault. Tense and frightened, they had continued to pour on the cross fire as they'd been doing until they realized better. He gazed between the wagons at the littered land beyond. The white wolf had countered with his own strategy, all too successfully. Fargo heard the long sigh that came from deep inside him.

Annabel pushed to her feet and came to him, her words echoing everyone else's questions. "What next?" she asked.

"We wait. Everybody stays in place," Fargo answered.

"How long?" she questioned.

His glance went to the moon and saw the pale white sphere growing close to the last of the mountain peaks. "Till day breaks, a few hours more," he said.

"Everyone's exhausted, really drained," she said.

"They can be drained or dead," he said harshly, and she took her place with the others beneath the wagons. He made no effort to soften his harshness. She had brought them all there with her stubbornness and her refusal to listen to advice and now it was all turning bad. He had tried, almost succeeded. The cross fire had taken its toll, but the wolf-pack leader had fought back and now he couldn't lose. Could he still save anybody, Fargo asked himself. He swore silently at the answer that shimmered inside him.

He lowered himself against the rear wheel of one of the wagons and saw Jake and Harry sit down nearby. His eyes slowly moved over the waiting figures under the wagons. Many had dozed off, the youngsters hard asleep. Vivian stared unblinkingly across the flat land, he saw, and Thomas Turner and Annabel spoke in half-whispered tones. He closed his eyes but only to let the rest of his senses grow more acute, and finally the wagons grew silent and he stayed with his head back against the wheel rim.

At least another hour had gone by when his eyes snapped open. It was nothing he'd heard but his own sixth sense going off inside him, that inner alarm called instinct. He whirled, his eyes narrowed, and peered out from under the wagons. The night had begun to drift into dawn and the morning mists were wispy tatters of gauze that floated across the clear space. But there was something more amid the mists, stealthy shapes that moved toward him on silent paws. They vanished into the mists, appeared again, more coming into view. No frontal charge this time, no more reckless plunge into the withering gunfire. Silence and stealth and the cloak of the morning mists.

"Wake up," he barked. "They're coming." He saw the others snap awake, bring their rifles up at once as they blinked out into the mists. "No cross fire this time. We don't have the ammunition left," he yelled. "They won't be charging in waves. Aim and shoot."

He motioned Jake and Harry to stay with him by the wagons and he saw the first four stealthy shapes suddenly appear, too close, moving in with swift silence. Another one appeared a half-dozen yards to the left, then two more behind it. He fired and one wolf went down and he listened to the gunfire erupt as the attackers came into sight, darting forward, flattening themselves and darting away. Three or four darted forward at a time, lots of space between them, swerving and darting away while another three sprang forward only to leap away as the gunfire erupted. They thrust with their bodies, flattened themselves, darted forward and away, in and out of the mists in pairs, individually, sometimes three and four but always with space between them.

But Annabel and the others kept up a steady barrage and he saw three, maybe five, attackers go down, and still the wolves kept darting forward only to dash back almost at once. They kept up the jabbing, thrusting attacks and a few more paid the price. But most escaped into the mists and Fargo heard Bettledorf's curse. "Goddamn, I'm out of ammunition," the man boomed, and there was both a terrible realization as well as anger in his voice.

"Me, too, dammit," Seth Crowler shouted as he threw down his rifle and yanked the gun from his holster.

"Save your six-gun," he shouted, and Crowler halted.

A shaft of morning sun cascaded across the mountaintop to send the mists scattering and Fargo saw the wolves turn at once and hurry back across the clearing. The sunlight quickly flooded the land.

Fargo rose and stepped out from beneath the wagons. He stared across the scattered bodies to the hillside and saw the majestic white wolf waiting, peering back at him. This time Fargo turned his back on the wolf and walked disdainfully back inside the circle.

But his gesture had a hollow core to it, he realized bitterly. He watched the others emerge from beneath the wagons. "How much ammunition do you have left?" he asked. Herb Starr had the most rifle shells left, an even dozen. The others were down to empty or not more than a few shells at best.

"They'll come at us again, now, won't they?" Lucy Harding said.

"Not till tonight," he said. "They don't know what we've left. They won't risk an attack in broad daylight."

"We just wait? Annabel asked.

"No, we get some sleep first, a full day's sleep," Fargo said. "Then, before dark, we move out. They'll just overrun us if we stay here."

"They'll attack, anyway, won't they?" Simon Crater asked.

"Yep, but you'll fight them off from inside your wagons and you'll be moving. That's the best I can offer. Maybe it'll be enough," Fargo said. It was a miserly hope, he realized, but he had nothing else. The dynamite sticks and the gunpowder in Annabel's wagon were a last resort. Maybe he'd never find a way to use them, but he'd not waste them either. He walked away, took his bedroll down, and was asleep in minutes.

Exhaustion let him sleep soundly until he woke with the midafternoon sun receding across the sky. He rose, heard the others waking, and went to the wagons and gazed across the flat land to the hillside. It was empty and he smiled. Another gesture had been given, another challenge flung. It would be taken, only the white wolf would not know why. He'd see it as defiance when it really was desperation. That irony would perhaps be their only victory, Fargo grunted bitterly as he turned back to where the others were preparing to move out.

He put his bedroll away and swung onto the Ovaro. The others stared at the empty hillside, not daring to hope yet unable not to do so. Twilight began to slip over the mountains as he rode forward alongside Annabel's wagon. He led the way back to the passage that stretched on through the rolling hillsides. The night came to give them another hour of safety until the full moon rose. The passage widened and remained level, Fargo saw, but thick tree cover edged both sides of it. He kept the wagons moving slowly as the moonlight filtered through the trees, and his lips drew back when he saw the dark shapes materialize in the trees. They moved down toward the wagons from both sides, he saw. He turned and rode back alongside the wagons. "When you've no more bullets left, use rakes, pitchforks, your rifles as clubs. Fight from inside your wagons and don't stop moving," he said. "Crater, you and Harry join one of the wagons. You'll be a sitting duck on a horse alone."

"Not me, Fargo," Simon said. "I'm getting out of here. It's every man for himself now." He slapped the reins against the horse's neck, dug boots into the steed's ribs, and sent the mount racing on.

"No, don't," Fargo called out. But Simon Crater was into a full gallop and Fargo saw the half-dozen shapes spring into action in the trees, become dark streaks. Crater rounded a slow turn in the passage when the sound of his scream echoed back, punctuated by a single shot and then another scream. Fargo saw Jake and Harry leap onto one of the wagons at once and he rode forward again, passed Vivian with a rifle at the tailgate of her wagon. She blew a kiss at him as he passed, and he slowed alongside Annabel, bringing the Ovaro close to the wagon. He swung from the saddle to the driver's seat. The Ovaro would stay with the wagon, he knew, and he met Annabel's frightened eyes as he took the reins from her.

"Get inside the wagon," he said. "Stay there." She nodded and crawled through the opening behind the driver's seat.

Fargo lay the big Sharps half on his lap and half on the seat. He snapped the reins and sent the horses into a run and cursed as the powerful howl exploded in the night. It seemed almost instantly that the gray-brown shapes charged from the trees on both sides, leaping up at the wagons. He peered back as he heard a half-dozen shots and saw two of the attackers fall by the roadside. But he saw two more vault onto the side of the Hardings' wagon, razor-sharp teeth ripping the canvas aside. Harding drove a rake into one, Fargo saw, and managed to kick the other away, but three more sprang onto the wagon. Fargo heard Harding scream, then Lucy Harding's voice join his—but only for a moment as snapping fangs sank into the back of her neck. He saw the horses swerve to the right and the wagon smash into kindling wood against the trees.

But the night had become a place of a few futile gunshots and the sound of screams and snarls, of dark shapes that leapt through canvas with the force of giant, furred lances. Some of the wagons ran into the trees as the horses panicked. He saw Bettledorf standing in the center of his driverless wagon, his hands around the throat of one wolf while two others leapt at him. He tore his eyes from the deadly struggles going on behind him as he glimpsed two wolves come up alongside him. The first one gathered itself and executed a flying leap that landed it at the edge of the driver's seat. Fargo pressed the trigger of the Sharps and the wolf hurtled into the air. The second one did the same and again he blew it from the wagon.

He'd only one more round in the rifle and he held his fire as another pair of wolves raced alongside but made no effort to leap aboard. The wagon suddenly rocked as three heavy thunks resounded against the closed sides, but the wood panels were thick enough and they held. Two more tried crashing through as they had with the canvas-sided wagons and fell away. He leaned to the right and peered behind him. Only one wagon raced after him, the canvas ripped apart and Seth Crowler's body hanging over the side, his head barely attached to his shoulders.

Fargo brought his eyes back to the passage that stretched under the moonlight in a slow, uphill curve. The land at his left rose sharply and he saw three wolves race up to the top, slow, and wait for him to pass below. He drew his Colt as the first one leapt and his shot blew a hole in the animal's chest as it flew through the air. Its body slammed into the side of the wagon as it fell, but Fargo was already firing at the second leaping form. The wolf's neck spouted red and it fell beside the wagon. The third one leapt, miscalculated, and hit the ground directly in front of him and he heard its scream of pain as the wagon wheels passed over its body.

But Fargo's eyes scanned the land to his right, desperately searching for the box canyon he had found when he'd explored the terrain only a few short days earlier. He'd begun to wonder if he had missed it in the scramble to stay alive when he spied it in the pale moonlight. He swerved the wagon in a sharp left, saw two more streaking shapes coming at him, and fired the last round in the Sharps. Both wolves did half-rolls across the ground before they lay still.

Fargo raced the wagon toward the rockbound box canyon, the entranceway just wide enough to admit the wagon with high walls of rock on both sides. With the Ovaro racing along beside him, he reached the small canyon and charged through the entranceway to rein to a screeching halt.

He quickly backed the wagon up into the entranceway, swung from the seat, and fired the Colt at the first three wolves that made for the entrance. They fell and rolled down the slope that led up to the canyon. Fargo saw another six come to a halt and he heard the sharp call he had come to know all too well. The six wolves backed away and Fargo saw the white form appear atop a ledge some fifty yards away. The wolf stayed, raised its head, and howled again, the sound of victory in the cry.

Fargo knocked on the rear door of the wagon. "Open up and come out," he said. He heard the door latch pulled open and Annabel fell from the wagon and into his arms. He looked at the strained whiteness of her face, even the apple cheeks somehow long and drawn.

"My God, you've no idea what it was like in there, not knowing what was going on, just hearing the screams and the snarls, the crash of their bodies against the wagon," she said.

"You wouldn't have liked seeing it any better," he told her.

"Who's left besides us?" she asked. His eyes answered and her hand flew to her mouth. "Oh, God," she murmured. Her eyes went to the hills and trees and she saw the wolves gathered around the pale-white form of their leader. "Why haven't they come to finish us off?" she asked.

"They will. They're taking a breather," Fargo said. His eyes went to the stone box canyon again.

The sides were too steep to come down, the only way in through the narrow entranceway, the small canyon itself an oblong box. "I'd hoped some of the others would be with us when we reached here," he said. "But the attack was too savage."

"We'll be trapped for sure if we go in there," Annabel said.

"They're waiting to see if that's what we'll do. They'll move in to finish us off the minute we do, and that's our only chance," Fargo said, and drew a frown. "We've got to draw them in after us and do our own trapping."

"How, in God's name?" Annabel asked.

"By timing everything just right. It's our only chance," he said. "Get the dynamite and the gunpowder."

She disappeared into the wagon and came out with the dynamite first. He unwrapped the eight sticks as she brought out the small keg of gunpowder. He lay four sticks of the dynamite on each side of the narrow stone entranceway, then took the stopper from the keg and laid a trail of gunpowder to all eight sticks. Making certain the gunpowder touched the fuses on the dynamite sticks, he climbed onto the wagon and motioned Annabel to take the reins.

"Head for the far end of the canyon in a straight line," he said, and as she drove, he poured a trail of gunpowder alongside the wagon. By the time Annabel reached the end of the small canyon, he had used all the gunpowder in the keg. "Turn the wagon around," he said, and when she had done so, he sat beside her, his eyes on the narrow entranceway. He loaded his last six bullets into the Colt as the first of the wolves carefully entered the narrow opening to the canyon. Others followed quickly and finally he saw the powerful white form. The wolf-pack leader halted in the entranceway, his head arching upward, imperiousness in his every movement.

Slowly, the wolf moved into the canyon and started toward the lone wagon at the other end. The gray-brown shapes fell into step slightly behind their leader. "He's curious. He gave me more credit than to trap myself," Fargo said. "You take the reins." He swung down from the wagon and used one of three wooden matches he had in his pocket to light the gunpowder. It sputtered at first, flared, and then began to burn, quickly turning into a flickering, smoking trail along the stone.

"Drive," Fargo hissed, and Annabel snapped the reins hard and the wagon moved forward. "Faster," he said as the powder trail took on speed. She snapped the reins again and the horses responded, the Ovaro trotting alongside.

Most of the wolves had turned to follow along behind the wagon, a few keeping pace with it on one side, but all avoided the strange, sputtering, smoking serpent that ran in a straight line across the stone. The great white wolf stayed alone to one side, Fargo saw, keeping pace yet keeping his distance. Fargo saw the gunpowder trail increase speed again as it leapt over itself.

"Faster, dammit, go all out," Fargo said. "If we're not through that entranceway before the gunpowder hits that dynamite, you can have your choice of being blown apart or torn apart."

Annabel leaned forward, slapping the reins hard across the horses' rumps. The pair bolted into a burst of speed. They were outrunning the burning gunpowder now but just slightly, Fargo saw. "Keep it up," he yelled. He drew the Colt as three of the wolves put on speed, veered outward, and then started to come in at the wagon. He fired off three shots and one wolf stumbled and dropped and the other two scattered. But another three came in to leap upward and he sent another burst of shots at them. Once again, one fell while the other two swerved. A heavy, thick-shouldered attacker appeared and leapt with thunderous speed. Fargo fired his last two shots point-blank at the hurtling form and saw the animal's forechest explode in red. The wolf's body hit the corner of the wagon, bounced, and landed on the rump of one of the horses before it hit the ground. The horses leapt forward with another burst of speed and Fargo saw the narrow entranceway only a few feet ahead.

His eyes went to the sputtering and smoking trail of gunpower, not more than six inches behind. The main part of the wolf pack followed, aware that it made little difference if they caught their quarry inside the canyon or outside it. Final victory was only minutes away. Fargo's eyes were riveted on the burning trail of gunpowder as Annabel sent the wagon charging through the narrow entranceway. They had just cleared the opening when the first dynamite stick went off, then the second, and a tremendous roar followed as the others exploded.

"Duck," Fargo yelled as pieces of rock cascaded all around them. The Ovaro had raced on and Annabel sent the wagon chasing after him until Fargo closed his hands over hers and pulled back on the reins.

He brought the wagon to a halt and turned to look back to where a plume of smoke and dust rose into the air behind the pile of rocks that now sealed the opening to the canyon. "I'd say it got most of them," Fargo murmured. "And those left will take a while to scramble out."

Annabel's head fell against his shoulder as he

drove the wagon on for another few thousand yards before he halted again. He swung to the ground and began to unhitch the horses.

"You'll ride one of them," he said. "You can put your things on the other. We're leaving the wagon. It'll slow us down too much."

She nodded and began to take clothes and a few personal things from the wagon. She stuffed everything into a travel bag and Fargo used one of her extra blankets to form an Indian saddle for her. Finally, her things tied onto what was now a packhorse, she swung onto the big bay and Fargo onto the Ovaro. He led the way down a steep mountainside as the night drifted into dawn, and when the sun rose, he found a thick arbor where the shade was deep, and set out his bedroll. Annabel folded herself into his arms and slept in minutes, shock and terror still etched on her face.

He woke when the sun had gone into the midafternoon and she stirred and finally pulled her eyes open. A brook gurgled nearby and he rose and washed, watching Annabel as she shed clothes and splashed the cool, refreshing water around her. She looked more beautiful than she had a right to look. Only the pain in her eyes revealed what she had been through.

When she dressed and he found a stand of wild cherry, she pulled words from deep inside her. "Maybe we should go back and look," she said. "Maybe someone's still alive. Maybe someone survived."

He shook his head slowly. "There was no one," he said. "Vivian's visions were right. Her premonitions came true."

"Not altogether. We're here," Annabel said.

"Altogether enough," he said bitterly. "And

we're not out of these mountains yet. I've a rifle without shells and an empty six-gun. We'll cut through the mountains. We don't need any wagon trails now."

He rose, pulled her to her feet, and led the way out of the cool arbor and started down a steep mountainside. He rode steadily and made good time when he finally halted with another hour of daylight still left. He dismounted and used the throwing knife still in his calf holster to sharpen a point on a length of almost straight branch.

"We'll need to eat," he said. He nodded to the mountain hares that bounded back and forth nearby, and waited, on his haunches. Finally one grew too bold. The makeshift spear hurtled through the air. "Dinner," Fargo muttered.

The knife came in handy again to skin the hare, and while Annabel made a fire, he fashioned a simple roasting spit. It was dark when they ate but the meal tasted delicious and finally he lay beside her on his bedroll and the fire burned itself out.

"Just hold me," she murmured, her softness pressed against him. "I keep wondering."

"Wondering what?" he asked.

"Whether I'll ever be able to forget," she said. "Smile again, make love again."

"Stop wondering. That won't help," he said. "You'll go on. The human spirit allows that. But it doesn't allow forgetting."

"No, no forgetting," she murmured. Soon she slept hard against him.

He stayed awake a spell longer and listened to the night and felt the uneasiness stab at him. Just a residue of past uneasiness, he wondered, everything still too recent? Or something more? He finally closed his eyes and slept until the morning sun woke him.

He sat up and Annabel pulled her eyes open and pushed from the bedroll, her beautifully cupped breasts sparkling in the sunlight. He rose, pulled on clothes, and had just finished dousing himself with water from his canteen when he heard the sound and he felt every inch of his body grow taut.

The growl was a low, rumbling sound that rolled across the forest glen as a thunderstorm rolls across the prairie. Fargo turned, slowly, and his eyes found the white form atop a small rise, the black eyes boring into him.

"My God," he heard Annabel gasp. He saw three other wolves appear, but they stayed back. This would be a single challenge, he saw. The white wolf had managed to crawl out of the canyon more quickly than he'd imagined possible, Fargo grimaced. He'd picked up the wagon and followed their scent from there. And now he'd come for the final victory that had been denied him.

"Tie the horses to the tree. Don't let them run and scatter," Fargo said to Annabel, his eyes still on the wolf. "You get on the Ovaro. If it goes wrong, you ride like hell."

The white wolf lifted his head and the tremendous howl rose into the air. Fargo drew the knife from its calf holster. The great white form suddenly bounded into the air but not directly at him. The wolf moved sideways, through a clump of brush, came into sight again with another great leap that landed him in still another cluster of shrubs, and Fargo's laugh was grim. The wolf was waiting to see if he'd draw fire, moving in quick, short bursts to protect himself. Again, the powerful body leapt into sight from the brush, another angled bound into the thick foliage of a clump of nearby trees.

Suddenly, satisfied, Fargo saw the white shape

flattened low to the ground, the wolf streaking directly at him. He turned, legs half-bent, the knife in one hand. He forced himself to wait and stare into the great jaws that opened. The wolf was almost on him when he flung himself sideways and felt the thick-shouldered body brush across the back of his legs as the wolf's leap carried him past.

Fargo hit the ground and rolled, sprang to his feet to see the wolf charging again, the two-inch-long fangs gleaming white. The wolf leapt again and once more Fargo flung himself aside at the very last second and felt the animal's hot breath go past his face. He regained his feet instantly and saw the wolf come at him again. The wolf wouldn't try another leap. He was too smart for that. He'd adjust to his foe's tactics. Again Fargo waited.

The wolf came at him, gathering speed, but this time he stayed on the ground. Fargo feinted to his left and the animal responded with instant reflexes, swerving to the left as Fargo leapt to his right. As the wolf swerved past him, Fargo jumped, his long arms closing around the wolf's neck. With a savage roar, the wolf spun, tried to dislodge him, but Fargo hung on and heard the click of the long fangs that tried to sink into his shoulder. But he was too close for the wolf to turn enough to reach him. As the animal furiously struggled to throw him off, Fargo's hand brought the knife up in a short arc. He felt the blade go through fur, into muscle and flesh. The wolf roared in pain, hurled himself onto his back, and Fargo felt his grip around the animal's throat come loose.

The wolf rolled, leapt away, and whirled, and Fargo saw the line of red, brilliant against the white fur, coursing down the side of the animal's neck. Fargo scrambled back, started to regain his feet when his heel caught on a length of forest vine. He went down and cursed as the wolf sprang forward, too close to avoid this time. Fargo rolled and cried out in pain as he felt the slashing fang tear into his side. He was still on his back when the wolf landed on him, but he managed to bring both hands up as he dropped the knife. He locked his fingers around the powerful throat as the wolf's jaws snapped at him, only inches from his face. With roaring snarls, the animal dug his back legs into the ground for leverage and Fargo smelled the foul odor of decayed flesh still clinging to the wolf's teeth as the snapping jaws came closer.

Using his last ounce of strength, the Trailsman managed to get one leg up enough to plant his foot on the ground, and with his own roar, he rolled the wolf over and off him. He brought his hands from the animal's throat as the wolf tore away. He dived sideways and picked up the throwing knife he didn't dare throw without a certainty of a vital hit. He half-ran, half-scooted backward as the wolf, on his feet again, came toward him. No roaring leaps this time, he saw with grim satisfaction. The wolf mixed new respect with hate now. The beast darted forward, drew back, darted in again, and suddenly kept coming. Fargo swiped with the knife and the wolf pulled his head back just in time to avoid the blow.

Fargo circled and felt the pain that coursed down the left side of his body. He suddenly made his own move, a half-leaping thrust with the knife. The wolf reacted at once, ducked his head away, but suddenly spun and charged, his head lowered. Fargo half-backed, halted, and brought the knife down in an effort to plunge it into the space between the black, flashing eyes. But the wolf's head movements were lightning-fast and Fargo saw his blow miss and knew he'd no time to try another. He threw himself sideways, but again he cursed in pain as the slashing fangs tore into his waist.

He hit the ground on his side, managed to get to one knee as the wolf hurled himself at him, letting the taste of the kill destroy prudence. Fargo flung himself forward, the knife held out in front of him as though it were a truncated lance. He felt it go deep into the animal's neck as the wolf impaled himself on it. But the force of the charge carried the wolf forward and Fargo felt himself hurled to the ground. He landed on his back, rolled, and saw the wolf halt, turn, stagger, shake his head, and back away. The wolf shook his head and neck again and Fargo saw the knife fall to the ground. He rose, moved forward, arms outstretched, and fought away the wave of weakness that came over him. He heard himself cursing aloud. He had missed the jugular. The knife hadn't struck a death blow. But he saw the wolf back away as he advanced. He reached the knife, scooped it up, and dropped to one knee as the weakness swept over him again.

His body seemed on fire, his one side a searing pain that wouldn't stop. But the left side of the wolf's neck had turned a deep red, he saw. His thrusting knife hadn't been a death blow but it had been a crippling one, serious enough to bring the wolf the same searing pain and weakness that he felt. Fargo pulled himself to his feet, swayed, then forced himself to stand as he faced the red-stained form in front of him. The white wolf growled again but held his place and Fargo made no move. Slowly, the wolf moved backward, moved back again, halted at the edge of a cluster of alders. He lifted his blood-soaked neck and his head tilted upward. The howl circled into the air, still powerful, still commanding, and then he turned and vanished into the trees.

It was over, Fargo realized, with no defeat and no victory, the last howl a concession of a fight well-fought, an agreement sealed with blood. The white wolf would find his own ways to heal wounds, nature's ways made of cool, clear water and the medicines of the earth.

Fargo felt his legs give out under him. He sank to his knees and was only dimly aware of Annabel's arms around him as he passed out.

He heard the song of birds first and he slowly pulled his eyes open. He was on a mossy bed, in another place, and he winced with pain as he moved. He blinked, focused, and saw Annabel kneel down at his side. "How long have I been here?" he asked.

"Since yesterday," she said. "I found the salve in your saddlebag and used some of my blouses as bandages."

He pushed himself up on his elbows. It hurt, but not so much that he couldn't stand it. "I'll be able to ride in another day," he said.

"There's no hurry. I've gotten real good with that spear you made." She smiled. "We're having guinea hen for supper."

He lay back and found a smile. "All right," he said. "Another few days and I'll be fit for riding."

"Good," she murmured. "I want that." He frowned at her. "Then you'll be fit enough to make love to me," she finished.

"Definitely," he murmured, and lay back. Annabel's breasts pressed against him as she curled up with him.

When night came, he thought he heard the distant call of a wolf as he lay half-awake. But he couldn't be sure. Perhaps it was only inside him. It was a call that would echo there for a long time, he knew.

LOOKING FORWARD!

**The following is the opening
section from the next novel in the exciting
Trailsman series from Signet:**

TRAILSMAN #89
TEXAS HELL COUNTRY

*The Texas Hill Country,
a few days before Christmas, 1859—
where the forests are teeming with wild pigs,
hungry bears, and desperate men . . .*

The bushy evergreen really didn't have a chance. For starters, the tree wasn't much taller than either of the big men standing before it. Likely they could have just pushed hard and toppled it, but the men were taking turns with a broadax as the December sun began to sag low toward the Hill Country of central Texas.

"These goddamn cedars are so bushy near the trunk that it's a day's work just to reach in there with an ax blade." Green-eyed, red-bearded, and built as stout as a bulldog, Thomas Jefferson Baker took another whack. A hand-sized chip flew out, struck a low branch, and dropped into the thin, stony soil.

"Should have brought a saw, I reckon. Then we could cut off some of the lower limbs and get in there and chop this down before it gets too dark." Taller

Excerpt from TEXAS HELL COUNTRY

than Baker but not as husky, black-bearded Skye Fargo took the ax and swung. The tree shuddered.

"If we was just clearin' some land, that'd be the way to do it," Baker agreed. "But we want this one as bushy as we can keep it. Greta'd never forgive me if we came back to the house with an ugly hacked-up Christmas tree."

Fargo nodded while making sure that the fringed buckskin jacket he'd shed was still close by, draped over a stump. It was a pure pleasure to be outdoors a couple days before Christmas and not need to wear much more than a flannel shirt. He'd finally made it south in time to enjoy a mild Texas winter.

"Yeah, that juniper ought to make a handsome tree once Greta strings it with popcorn and puts a few candles on it."

Baker finished his swing before turning to Fargo. "Long as I've known you, Skye, I know better'n to call you a liar. But why for are you calling this a juniper? Everybody knows it's just a cedar."

Fargo took his own swing, and the tree began to topple as the men stepped back. "Tom, you can call it whatever you want to call it. You Texans seem to do things pretty much your own way, no matter what anybody else does. But the fact is, that's a Mexican juniper, not a cedar."

Baker turned to face the Trailsman. "Hell, cedar's all I ever heard 'em called."

"Sniff one of the chips, Tom," Fargo replied. "It won't smell like a cedar chest. Besides, see those little blue berries? Crush one and take a whiff. Smells just like English gin, which stands to reason because they use juniper berries for flavor."

Baker scooped up a chip and some berries. "I'll be damned, Skye. You're right. But it sure looks like

Excerpt from TEXAS HELL COUNTRY

a real cedar, what with those little green web leaves."

Fargo nodded. "Really can't blame folks for calling those junipers cedars, even if real cedars don't grow hereabouts." He paused. "What's next? Drag this back to your house so Greta can start to work on it?"

"Got another hour or so of light," Baker said, "so we don't exactly need to rush ourselves." He picked up a piece of grass rope, about twenty feet long, and tied it to the base of the downed tree.

As the two old friends caught up on each other, they strolled leisurely, tree in tow, toward Baker's farmstead, over on the other side of a small rise in this rolling timbered country.

Tom Baker had been surprised as hell to see Skye Fargo, the Trailsman, earlier this afternoon. Just as the farmer was stepping out of his substantial log barn, ax in hand for fetching a Christmas tree, up rode a tall man, muscled but whipcord-lean. He sat easily astride an Ovaro stallion whose gleaming white midsection was framed by jet-black fore and hindquarters.

As soon as Baker recognized him, Fargo was invited to put the Ovaro in a stall in the barn, and he joined Tom Baker on the jaunt to fetch a Christmas tree.

Skye Fargo had been heading south and west, down from Missouri after some business near Kansas City. After more than a month of tense riding through Indian country, the comfortable, almost luxurious Nimitz Hotel in Fredericksburg seemed as good a place as any to lay up for a couple days. Most of the local talk was in the guttural native speech of the German emigrants who populated this part of

Excerpt from TEXAS HELL COUNTRY

Texas, but he heard enough English to put two and two together.

It seemed that about seven years before, Greta Gottlieb, the beautiful blond daughter of a prosperous hardware merchant in San Antonio, had shocked everyone by marrying a re-bearded American, rather than a fellow German. And when Fargo discovered that the groom was named Baker, he made inquiries about finding the couple at the farm that they were carving out of the rock-strewn countryside.

The Trailsman carried fond memories of Greta. Her relatives and neighbors would doubtless be a lot more shocked if they had known just how warm-natured she had been back when Fargo had first met her during a fiesta down in San Antonio. Greta Gottlieb, though, had wanted to settle down and raise a family with a strong, hardworking man. Skye Fargo was as strong as they came, and he never backed off from work that had to be done, but he was the kind of man who'd never settle down, even with a woman like Greta.

In those days, Tom Baker wasn't exactly the settling type, either. He and the Trailsman had ridden together on one of the meanest jobs in the West. The Butterfield Stage Line generally carried the U.S. mail and up to a dozen uncomfortable passengers for thirteen hundred miles between San Antonio, Texas, and San Diego, California. The sunbaked desert trip took four weeks that seemed like eternity. On account of the Comanche and Apache, each trip required six armed escorts.

For a few months, Fargo and Tom Baker had been among those forty-dollar-a-month escorts. One blistering morning in San Diego, Fargo had been offered other work, trailing Mexican cattle north to San Francisco. He took it. Tom Baker had figured it was

Excerpt from TEXAS HELL COUNTRY

time to quit, too. But he made one last run, back to San Antonio, a town he liked, and the two men hadn't seen each other since then.

"So they call you the Trailsman now?" Baker asked as they neared the house, its windows glowing in the twilight.

"Among other things." Fargo chuckled as they swung to their right to avoid dragging a tree through Greta's dormant garden. "Looks like you're doing well for yourself here."

Like many Texas houses, this one was built of logs, although it was chinked more tightly than most. The homestead was really two structures that sat a few paces apart. They were connected by a covered walkway that inspired folks to call these "dogtrot houses." Baker's had grown some recently with a new lean-to on one side. That must be where they'd put the kitchen, since blue-gray smoke rose from the stone chimney.

"Can't complain," Baker said. "We clear a little more land every year. Raise a few cattle, run a few hogs, grow some corn and this and that, and we get by."

"More than get by," Fargo said, noting a quick-moving low silhouette pass a window. "Either you've got a trick dog that walks on its hind legs, or you and Greta have a family now."

Even in the near-darkness, Baker's smile showed. "That little hellion is William Barret Travis Baker. He just turned six."

"So you named your son after the commander at the Alamo," Fargo commented. "That's sure a mouthful for a name, but I suppose when you go Texas, you go all the way."

"Something like that." Baker chuckled. "We just call him Billy, though, unless he's in trouble. Which happens often enough." Only steps from the door, the husky man halted.

So did Fargo. There was a muted crackle, followed by rustling in the trees, about a hundred yards off, back the way they'd just come. Fargo's hand dropped to the heavy colt revolver that never left his side. He started to crouch and felt Baker's hand on his shoulder.

"It's too dark, Skye. And like as not it don't mean nothin'."

Fargo straightened. "Happen before?"

"You hear brush sounds out here all the time. Lately things have been a little spooky, though. Remember how it was that night before the Apache attacked us on the other side of El Paso? Had that feeling you were being watched but you couldn't put your finger on anything?"

Fargo muttered agreement.

"That's how this has been for the past couple months. Get that feeling every now and again, but there never seems to be anything to it."

"Nosy neighbors, maybe?"

"We're the only house for four or five miles any which way," Baker explained. "Maybe it's just wild pigs in the brush."

"Javelinas are either real noisy or they don't make any sound," Fargo grunted. "Sounded two-legged to me."

"Well, you've got folks moving through here that are trying to stay hidden. Slaves that manage to escape from the cotton plantations to the east sometimes come through here, sneaking their way to Mexico, where they'll be free."

Fargo nodded. That made sense. Considering the substantial bounties of two or three hundred dollars that were posted on escaped slaves, a fugitive

Excerpt from TEXAS HELL COUNTRY

wouldn't be likely to cause any trouble. He'd just want to stay hidden. But still, it was irksome to see how Tom Baker, once so curious and adventuresome, was getting so settled these days that he wouldn't even investigate strange noises near his house.

"Talk to the local law about this?" Fargo wondered.

"Isn't any worth mention. There's a sheriff over to Fredericksburg, but he don't get out this way much."

"Texas Rangers?"

"They'd take care of it, for sure. But the Comanche are fractious to the north and west, out along the frontier, so that's where all the Rangers are."

"Could it be Comanche in your brush? Don't they still roam hereabouts?"

"Not enough to matter. When the Germans started to settle around here, back before our time here—it'd be '47, I reckon—their head man, John Meusebach, made a deal with the Penatka Comanche. Both sides have held to it pretty good. Comanche don't get along so good with the rest of Texas, but we manage here."

Obviously tired of speculating, Baker started moving again, toward the long front porch of his dogtrot house. After they set the tree on the porch, they stepped inside.

Fargo didn't quite know which felt better—the smell of a decent meal, or the way that tiny Greta nearly toppled him with a long embrace for an old friend.

"Skye, Skye, I cannot believe it is really you. What a Christmas present to have you visit us." Her long golden hair was done up in braids that she had pinned 'round atop her head, and she wore a patched

Excerpt from TEXAS HELL COUNTRY

and splattered apron that nearly reached the scrubbed plank floor. Since he'd last seen her, she had added a few pounds, mostly in the right places. Greta still looked and felt mighty good.

Seeing as she was now a married woman with her husband and son beside her, the Trailsman tried to ignore the stirring that came when Greta's ample bosom pressed against his abdomen as she nestled her head against his chest for a moment.

Besides, Fargo had other desires. At the moment, the Trailsman felt hungry enough to skin a dead skunk and start chewing. Greta returned to the cast-iron cook stove in the back room. Fargo found a chair, its seat covered with tanned deer hide, and relaxed. He leaned back, savoring the pungent aroma of spicy sausage frying with potatoes.

Most everywhere else in the Lone Star State, meals consisted of greasy bacon and chunky corn pone—breakfast, dinner, and supper. Even though Texans considered pecans fit for hog feed and not much else, Fargo found the nuts a welcome relief from the state's usual fare. And a cheap one, since pecan trees were almost as common as the "cedars."

Little Billy started to disturb the Trailsman's comfortable languor, but his father shushed him after only a few chatters. General silence continued through the hearty dinner. Once Greta had hauled the plates away, though, everyone opened up, especially when she brought out a bottle of wine that a neighbor had put up from local wild grapes.

Billy seemed impressed by the tall visitor, although his face fell when he learned that Skye Fargo was not a Texas Ranger.

"But you know Rangers, don't you?" the boy asked.

Fargo smiled. Billy had his dad's red hair and

Excerpt from TEXAS HELL COUNTRY

stocky build, with his mother's chin, nose, and mouth. "Sure, Billy, I know a few Rangers. Even rode with them a time or two."

"Really?"

Fargo told a few tales without stretching the truth much, about what he'd been doing the past few years.

"Won't you ever settle down?" Greta wondered.

"The day may come," Fargo granted. "And a man could do a lot worse than what you folks have managed. But there's things that gnaw at a man and just won't let him rest."

Tom and Greta's eyes met Fargo's. They knew his past. When not much more than a boy, Skye Fargo had visited away from home—a remote Wells Fargo stage station run by his father. During his absence, two raiding men had burned the station and butchered the family. The young man who returned to the ruins and the slaughter changed his name to Skye Fargo and vowed to search for the culprits. Until he found them and dealt them justice, he couldn't ever settle.

There was no sense discussing that in front of the boy, so Greta changed the subject.

"Billy, it is time for bed."

Tom stifled a yawn and added, "In fact, it's time for all of us to get some shut-eye. There's plenty to do tomorrow."

With doleful eyes, the boy examined the ladder that led upstairs to the loft above the main room.

"Please, Mama, can't I stay up and listen to more of Mr. Fargo's stories?"

She shook her head. "No. Maybe tomorrow.'

If the boy had moved any slower, he'd have been going backward, but eventually he got up to the loft.

"What's the plan here?" Fargo wondered aloud.

Excerpt from TEXAS HELL COUNTRY

"I can bring in my bedroll and bunk up there with him."

Tom looked relieved as Greta nodded and said that would be fine.

"Before I bed down, though, I want to borrow a lantern," the Trailsman said. "Finding my bedroll and the rest of my possibles in an unfamiliar barn could be tricky in the dark. Besides, I just recalled that I left my jacket where we cut the tree."

"I can come along and show you the way." Tom rose to fetch a coal-oil lantern.

"No, I can handle it fine." Fargo got up and beat his host to the lantern. He turned and winked. "Best you not waste any time getting into bed."

Tom Baker sported a ruddy complexion anyway, and the waving orange light from the room's only lamp reddened him. So it was hard to be sure whether the man was blushing. "Yep," he finally said. "Bed does sound a sight more comfortable than fetching that jacket. See you in the morning, Skye."

The jacket was simply an excuse to get out of the house for a spell. Fargo could almost feel the tension inside. Something wasn't sitting right with Tom Baker.

Maybe it was the prowlers or whatever that he had been sensing that made him seem edgy. More likely it was the presence of Skye Fargo, a man who had spent considerable time around Greta back when he was in and out of San Antonio on a regular basis.

That liaison was long past over. Fargo and Greta were friends and nothing more these days. But no man Fargo knew—and the Trailsman didn't think that if the time ever came he'd be an exception—ever felt entirely comfortable around any other man who'd once been close to his wife.

So he and Tom Baker would both likely feel better

Excerpt from TEXAS HELL COUNTRY

if the Trailsman rode on tomorrow. Fargo could reach New Braunfels easily, maybe even San Antonio. It wouldn't be the first Christmas he'd spent alone and moving on. Visiting old friends had seemed like such a good idea yesterday. He and Tom had once been close as brothers, but a lot had gone by since then. As much as it sometimes pained you, you just had to let it go by.

Guided by starlight and a sliver of moon, Fargo found the buckskin jacket quickly enough. He didn't light the lantern until his return trip, when he reached the general area where those rustling and crackling sounds had come from earlier.

Under a moss-ridden post oak, the Trailsman found human tracks. They didn't stand to reason. An escaping slave would likely be going barefoot, even in December. Comanches wore moccasins. The impressions, barely visible in the thin soil, had been formed by boots. But the heels spread too wide and the toes ran too broad to be the boots worn by Texans. Something like army boots, from the look of them.

Further study showed that there were two men in such boots that had been lurking there this afternoon. Their perch gave them a good view of the dogrun cabin while allowing the men to stay out of sight behind some brush. From the length of their paces, Fargo judged that the men had been about the same height and weight—about five-eight and one hundred sixty pounds. Just about average, both of them.

But what the hell were they doing spying on Tom Baker? And what, Skye frowned, was he going to do about it?

SIGNET WESTERNS BY JON SHARPE (0451)

RIDE THE WILD TRAIL

- [ ] THE TRAILSMAN #57: FORTUNE RIDERS (144945—$2.75)
- [ ] THE TRAILSMAN #58: SLAUGHTER EXPRESS (145240—$2.75)
- [ ] THE TRAILSMAN #59: THUNDERHAWK (145739—$2.75)
- [ ] THE TRAILSMAN #60: THE WAYWARD LASSIE (146174—$2.75)
- [ ] THE TRAILSMAN #62: HORSETHIEF CROSSING (147146—$2.75)
- [ ] THE TRAILSMAN #63: STAGECOACH TO HELL (147510—$2.75)
- [ ] THE TRAILSMAN #64: FARGO'S WOMAN (147855—$2.75)
- [ ] THE TRAILSMAN #66: TREACHERY PASS (148622—$2.75)
- [ ] THE TRAILSMAN #67: MANITOBA MARAUDERS (148908—$2.75)
- [ ] THE TRAILSMAN #68: TRAPPER RAMPAGE (149319—$2.75)
- [ ] THE TRAILSMAN #69: CONFEDERATE CHALLENGE (149645—$2.75)
- [ ] THE TRAILSMAN #70: HOSTAGE ARROWS (150120—$2.75)
- [ ] THE TRAILSMAN #71: RENEGADE REBELLION (150511—$2.75)
- [ ] THE TRAILSMAN #72: CALICO KILL (151070—$2.75)
- [ ] THE TRAILSMAN #73: SANTA FE SLAUGHTER (151399—$2.75)
- [ ] THE TRAILSMAN #74: WHITE HELL (151933—$2.75)
- [ ] THE TRAILSMAN #75: COLORADO ROBBER (152263—$2.75)
- [ ] THE TRAILSMAN #76: WILDCAT WAGON (152948—$2.75)
- [ ] THE TRAILSMAN #77: DEVIL'S DEN (153219—$2.75)
- [ ] THE TRAILSMAN #78: MINNESOTA MASSACRE (153677—$2.75)
- [ ] THE TRAILSMAN #79: SMOKY HELL TRAIL (154045—$2.75)
- [ ] THE TRAILSMAN #80: BLOOD PASS (154827—$2.95)
- [ ] THE TRAILSMAN #82: MESCALERO MASK (156110—$2.95)
- [ ] THE TRAILSMAN #83: DEAD MAN'S FOREST (156765—$2.95)
- [ ] THE TRAILSMAN #84: UTAH SLAUGHTER (157192—$2.95)
- [ ] THE TRAILSMAN #85: CALL OF THE WHITE WOLF (157613—$2.95)

Prices slightly higher in Canada

Buy them at your local

bookstore or use coupon

on next page for ordering.

ⓛ SIGNET (0451)

WILD, WILD WESTERNS

☐ **COLTER by Quint Wade.** Colter's brother was gunned down in a hellhole Arizona town, and nothing was going to stop Colter from finding his killer . . . not the hired guns who left him for dead, not the sheriff who told him to clear out, not even the cold-as-steel cattle baron who owned everyone in town. But lots of men were going to stop his bullets as he blazed a trail to the truth. . . . (151925—$2.75)

☐ **KENYON by Quint Wade.** Kenyon had his work cut out for him. There was his greenhorn sidekick who couldn't stay out of trouble. There were the widows putting their lives on the line to save their land. There was a land-grabbing cattle king and his cutthroat crew. And then there was Wingate, the most feared gunfighter in the West, who was in town to cut Kenyon down . . . (154053—$2.75)

☐ **THE KINCAIDS by Matt Braun.** They tamed an untamed land—but not the passions raging within them. Over three generations and tens of thousands of Western wilderness acres, theirs was the kingdom, the power, and the glory of the American dream. . . . (153693—$4.50)

☐ **BLACK FOX by Matt Braun.** A thunderous saga of West Texas aflame—when men and women fought against all odds. Three men, their women and their children matching courage against courage as they fought the fiercest tribes in the West. . . . (155572—$3.50)

Prices slightly higher in Canada

Buy them at your local bookstore or use this convenient coupon for ordering.

NEW AMERICAN LIBRARY
P.O. Box 999, Bergenfield, New Jersey 07621

Please send me the books I have checked above. I am enclosing $_____
(please add $1.00 to this order to cover postage and handling). Send check or money order—no cash or C.O.D.'s. Prices and numbers are subject to change without notice.

Name_____
Address_____
City _____ State _____ Zip Code _____

Allow 4-6 weeks for delivery.
This offer is subject to withdrawal without notice.